MERCER MAYER'S CRITTER KIDS® ADVENTURES

THE JAGUAR PAW PUZZLE

A GRAPHIC NOVEL ADVENTURE

#4

School Specialty Publishing

Copyright © 2006 © 1995 Mercer Mayer Ltd.
Text for Page 32 © 2006 School Specialty Publishing.
Published by School Specialty Publishing, a member of the School Specialty Family.
A Big Tuna Trading Company, LLC/J. R. Sansevere Book
Originally published as Jaguar Paw.

Written by Erica Farber/J. R. Sansevere
Special thanks to Professor Mary Miller, Chair, Department of the History of Art, Yale University
ISBN 0-7696-4765-0
1 2 3 4 5 6 7 8 9 10 PHX 11 10 09 08 07 06

The **MAYA** civilization began around 1000 B.C. in Mexico and Central America. Between 800 and 900 A.D., the Maya mysteriously left their cities and temples.

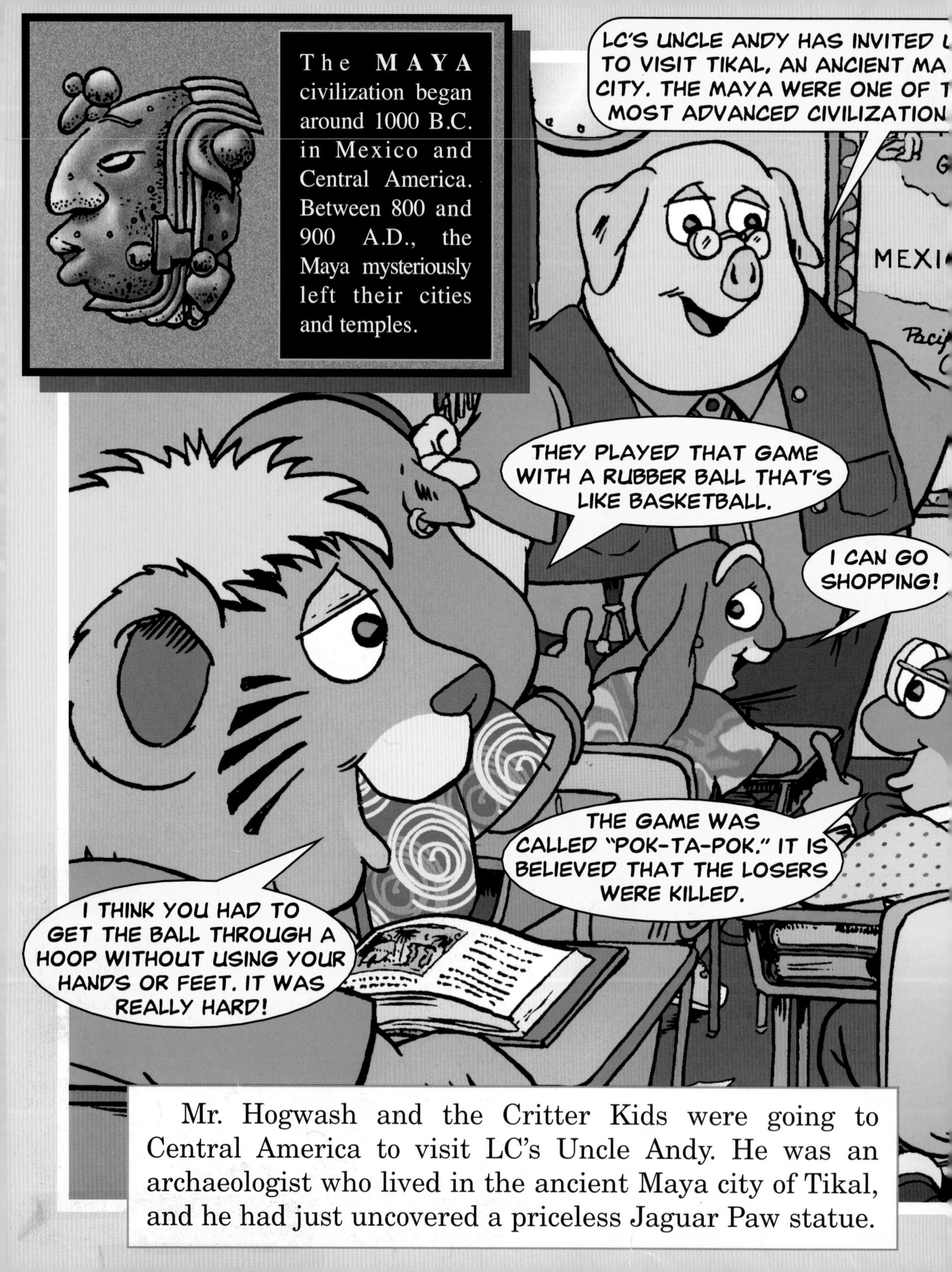

LC'S UNCLE ANDY HAS INVITED
TO VISIT TIKAL, AN ANCIENT
CITY. THE MAYA WERE ONE OF
MOST ADVANCED
MEXI
THEY PLAYED THAT GAME WITH A RUBBER BALL THAT'S LIKE BASKETBALL.
I CAN GO SHOPPING!
I THINK YOU HAD TO GET THE BALL THROUGH A HOOP WITHOUT USING YOUR HANDS OR FEET. IT WAS REALLY HARD!
THE GAME WAS CALLED "POK-TA-POK." IT IS BELIEVED THAT THE LOSERS WERE KILLED.

Mr. Hogwash and the Critter Kids were going to Central America to visit LC's Uncle Andy. He was an archaeologist who lived in the ancient Maya city of Tikal, and he had just uncovered a priceless Jaguar Paw statue.

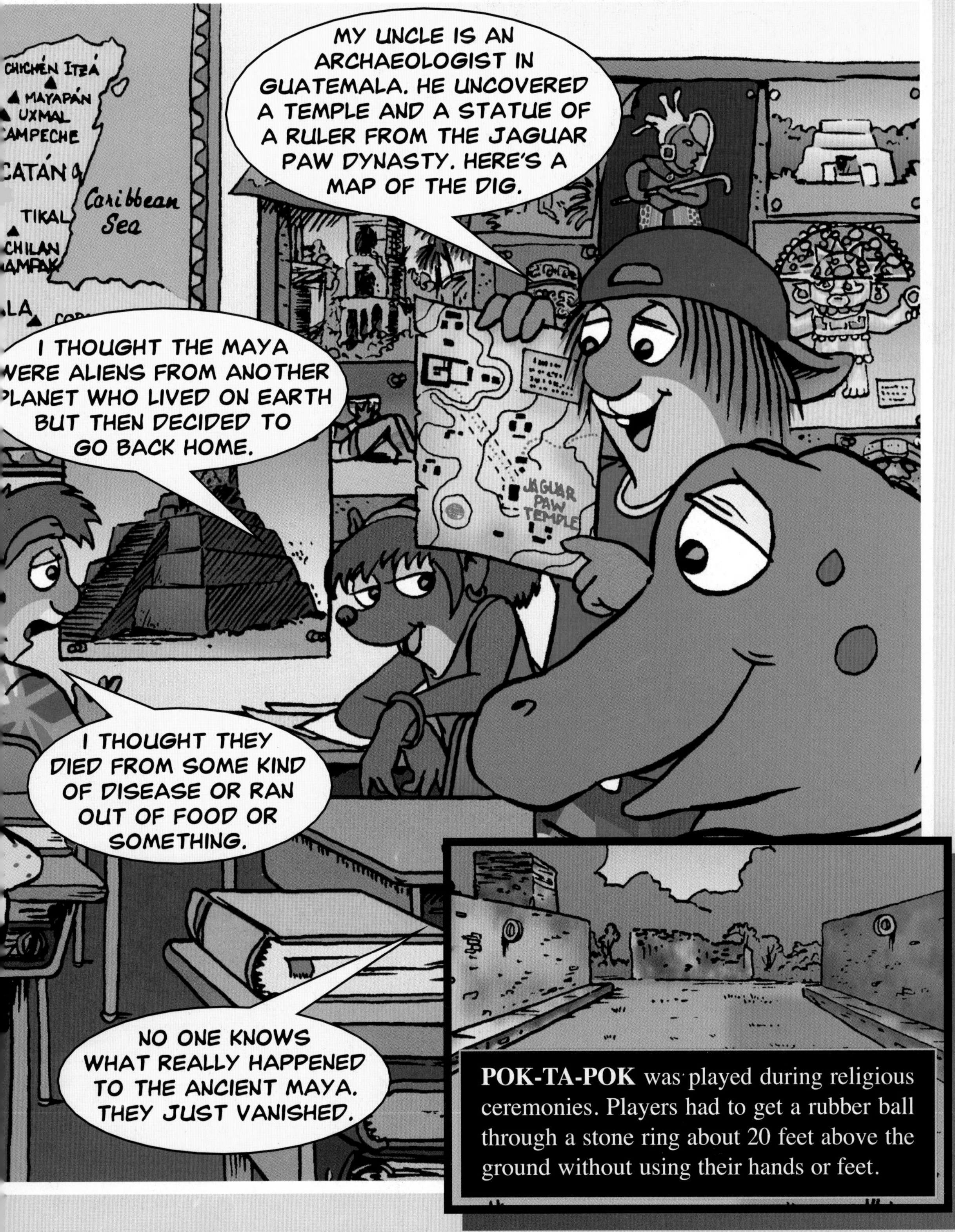
CHICHÉN ITZÁ
MAYAPÁN
UXMAL
Caribbean Sea
TIKAL
MY UNCLE IS AN ARCHAEOLOGIST IN GUATEMALA. HE UNCOVERED A TEMPLE AND A STATUE OF A RULER FROM THE JAGUAR PAW DYNASTY. HERE'S A MAP OF THE DIG.
JAGUAR PAW TEMPLE
I THOUGHT THE MAYA WERE ALIENS FROM ANOTHER PLANET WHO LIVED ON EARTH BUT THEN DECIDED TO GO BACK HOME.
I THOUGHT THEY DIED FROM SOME KIND OF DISEASE OR RAN OUT OF FOOD OR SOMETHING.
NO ONE KNOWS WHAT REALLY HAPPENED TO THE ANCIENT MAYA. THEY JUST VANISHED.

POK-TA-POK was played during religious ceremonies. Players had to get a rubber ball through a stone ring about 20 feet above the ground without using their hands or feet.

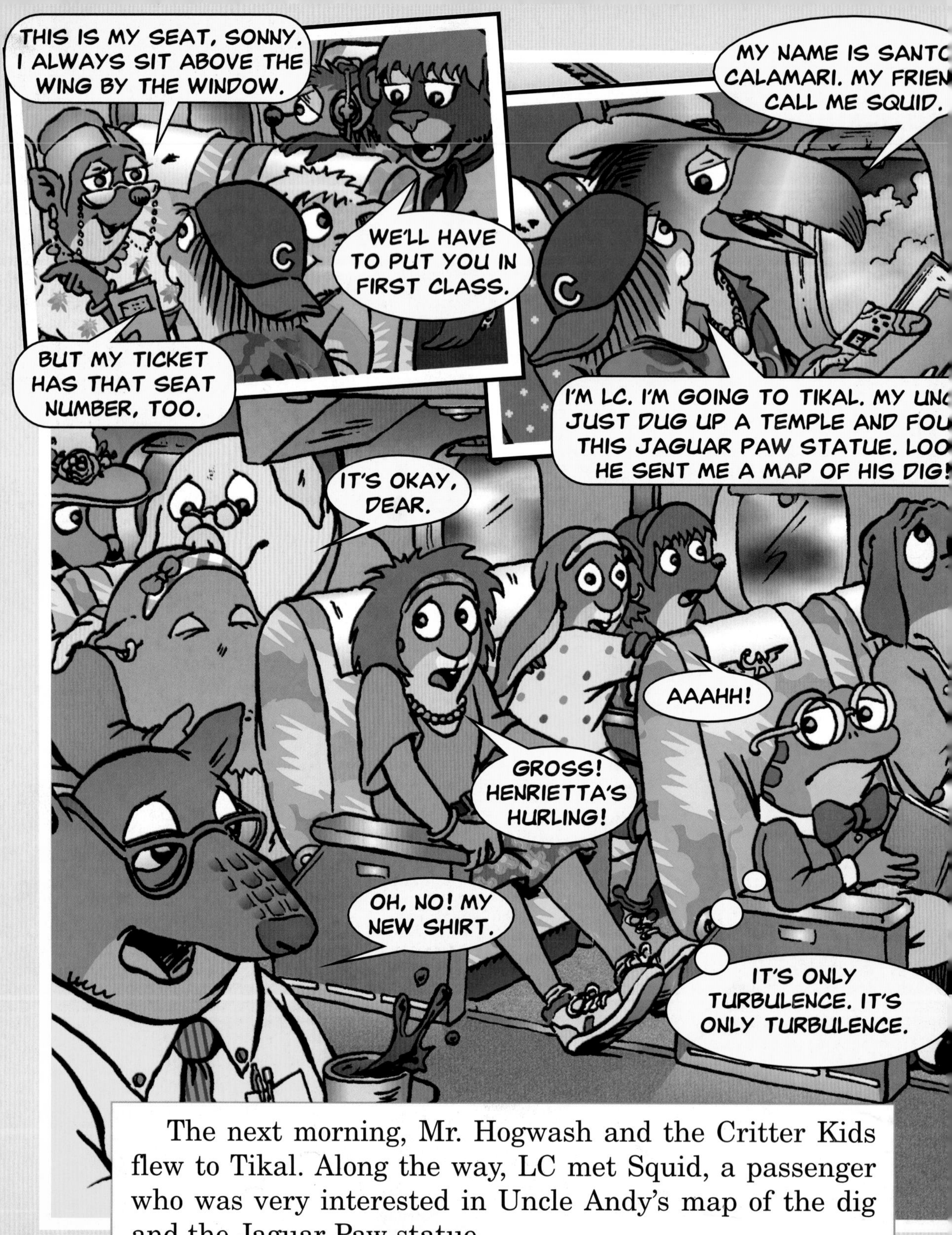
THIS IS MY SEAT, SONNY. I ALWAYS SIT ABOVE THE WING BY THE WINDOW.
BUT MY TICKET HAS THAT SEAT NUMBER, TOO.
WE'LL HAVE TO PUT YOU IN FIRST CLASS.
MY NAME IS SANTO CALAMARI. MY FRIEN CALL ME SQUID.
I'M LC. I'M GOING TO TIKAL. MY UNC JUST DUG UP A TEMPLE AND FOU THIS JAGUAR PAW STATUE. LOO HE SENT ME A MAP OF HIS DIG!
IT'S OKAY, DEAR.
AAAHH!
GROSS! HENRIETTA'S HURLING!
OH, NO! MY NEW SHIRT.
IT'S ONLY TURBULENCE. IT'S ONLY TURBULENCE.

The next morning, Mr. Hogwash and the Critter Kids flew to Tikal. Along the way, LC met Squid, a passenger who was very interested in Uncle Andy's map of the dig and the Jaguar Paw statue.

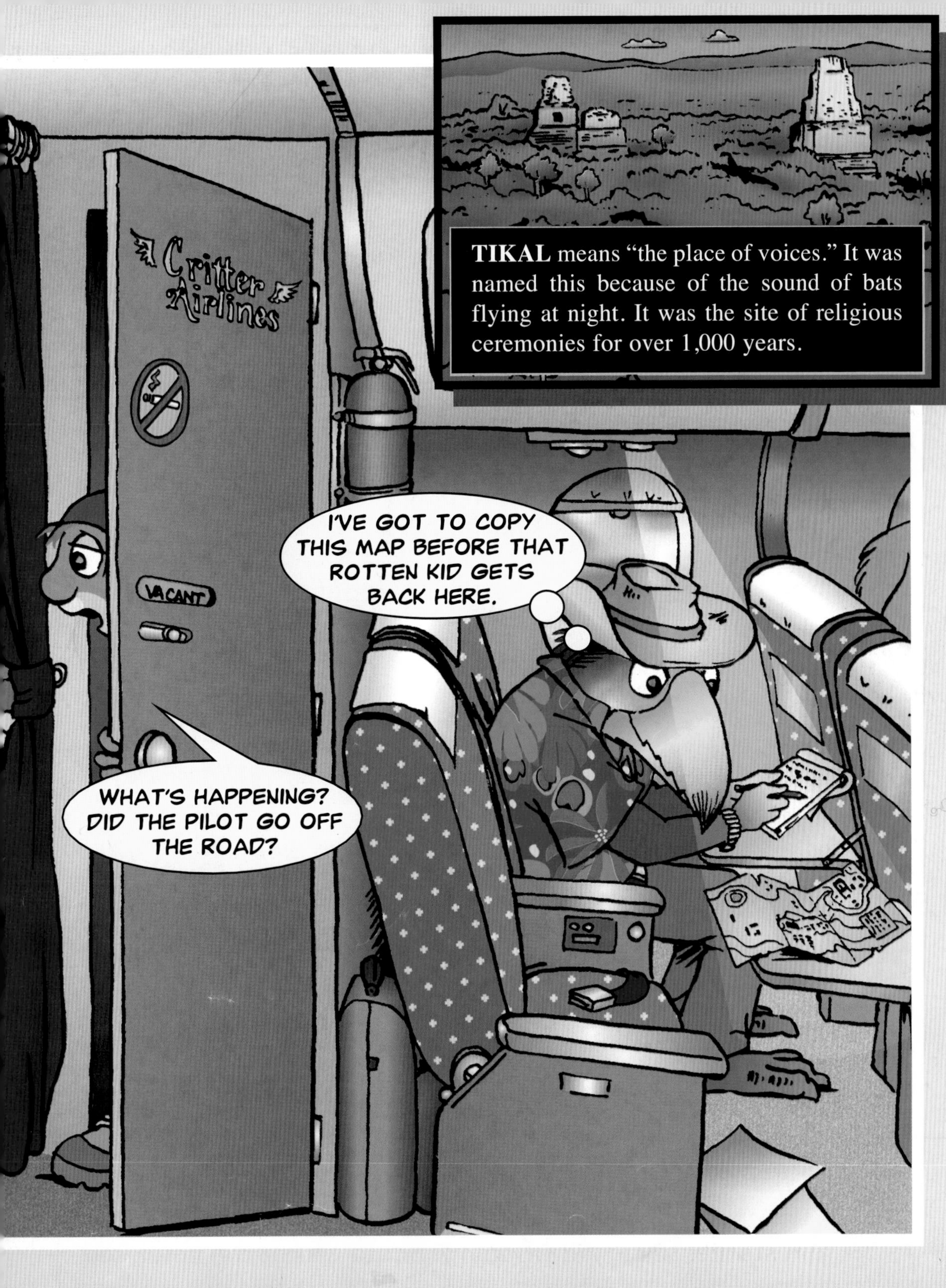

TIKAL means "the place of voices." It was named this because of the sound of bats flying at night. It was the site of religious ceremonies for over 1,000 years.
Critter Airlines
VACANT
I'VE GOT TO COPY THIS MAP BEFORE THAT ROTTEN KID GETS BACK HERE.
WHAT'S HAPPENING? DID THE PILOT GO OFF THE ROAD?

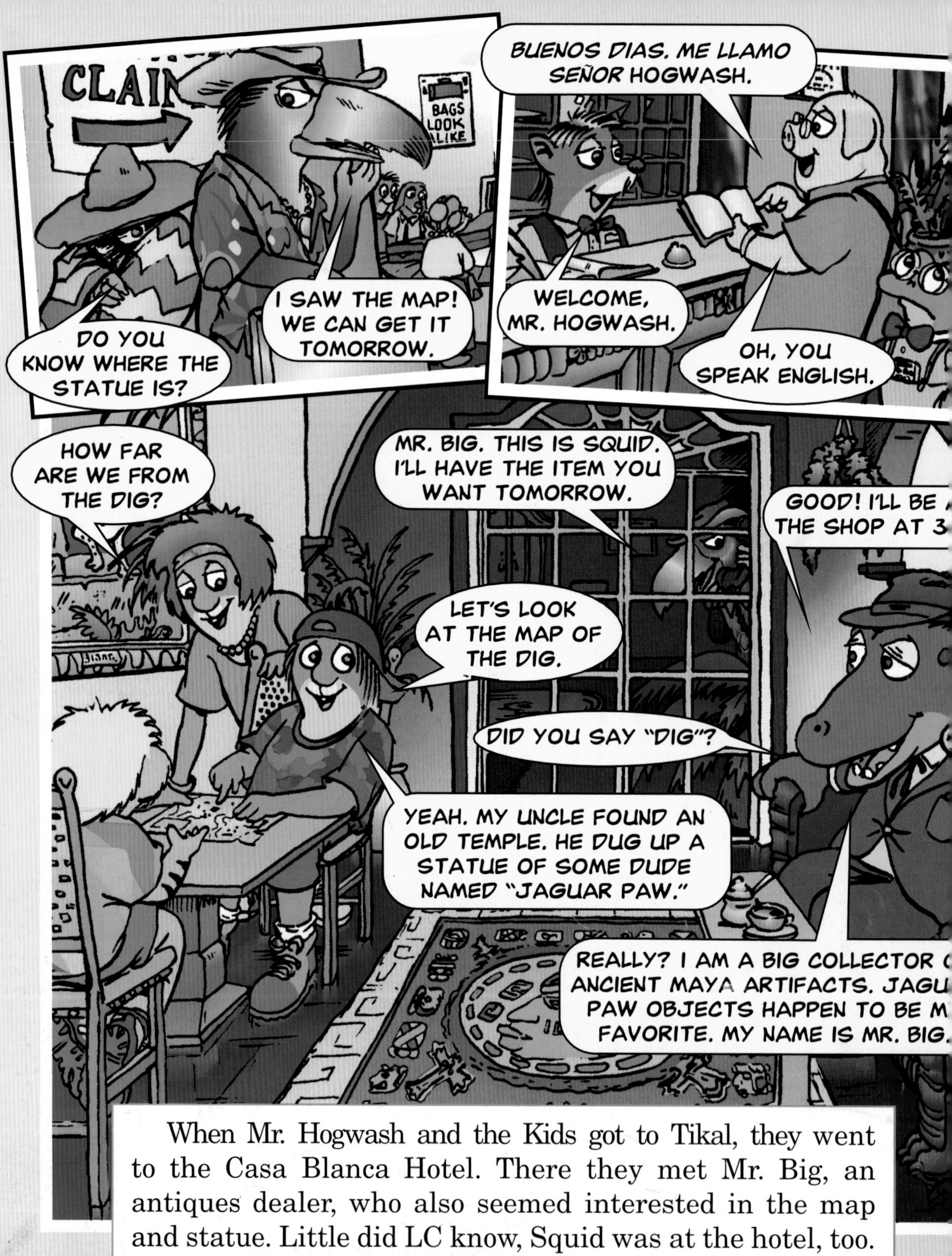
CLAI
BAGS LOOK ALIKE
DO YOU KNOW WHERE THE STATUE IS?
I SAW THE MAP! WE CAN GET IT TOMORROW.
BUENOS DIAS. ME LLAMO SEÑOR HOGWASH.
WELCOME, MR. HOGWASH.
OH, YOU SPEAK ENGLISH.
HOW FAR ARE WE FROM THE DIG?
MR. BIG. THIS IS SQUID. I'LL HAVE THE ITEM YOU WANT TOMORROW.
GOOD! I'LL BE A
THE SHOP AT 3
LET'S LOOK AT THE MAP OF THE DIG.
DID YOU SAY "DIG"?
YEAH. MY UNCLE FOUND AN OLD TEMPLE. HE DUG UP A STATUE OF SOME DUDE NAMED "JAGUAR PAW."
REALLY? I AM A BIG COLLECTOR O
ANCIENT MAYA ARTIFACTS. JAGU
PAW OBJECTS HAPPEN TO BE M
FAVORITE. MY NAME IS MR. BIG.

When Mr. Hogwash and the Kids got to Tikal, they went to the Casa Blanca Hotel. There they met Mr. Big, an antiques dealer, who also seemed interested in the map and statue. Little did LC know, Squid was at the hotel, too.

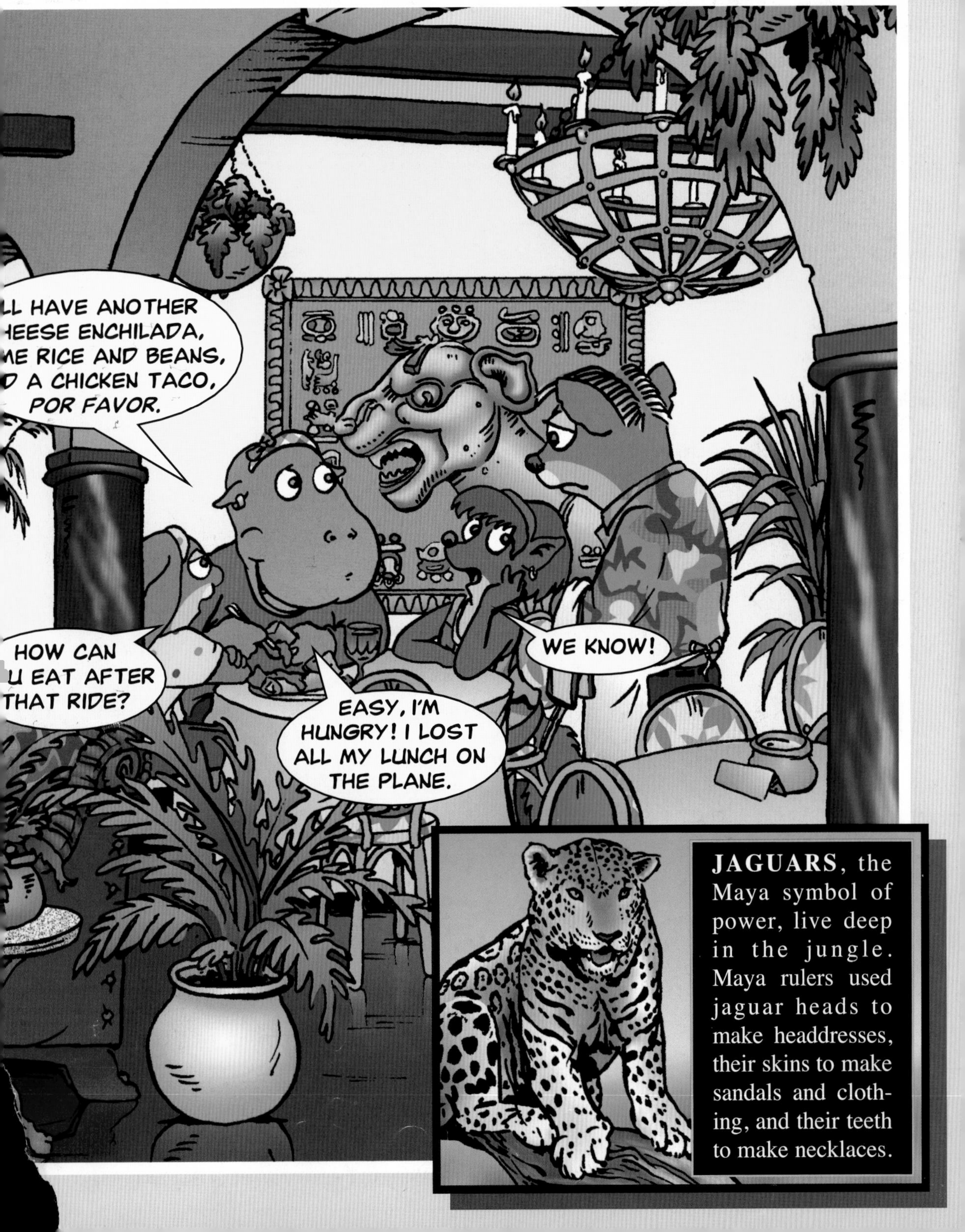
LL HAVE ANOTHER HEESE ENCHILADA, ME RICE AND BEANS, D A CHICKEN TACO, POR FAVOR.
HOW CAN U EAT AFTER THAT RIDE?
EASY, I'M HUNGRY! I LOST ALL MY LUNCH ON THE PLANE.
WE KNOW!

JAGUARS, the Maya symbol of power, live deep in the jungle. Maya rulers used jaguar heads to make headdresses, their skins to make sandals and clothing, and their teeth to make necklaces.

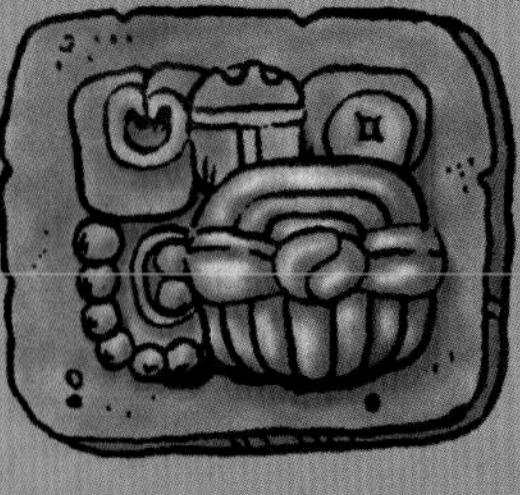

The highlighted symbol is the glyph for the city of **TIKAL**.

The Maya were the only New World culture to have a written language as complex as ours. Their alphabet was made up of 492 **GLYPHS**, symbols representing words or sounds.

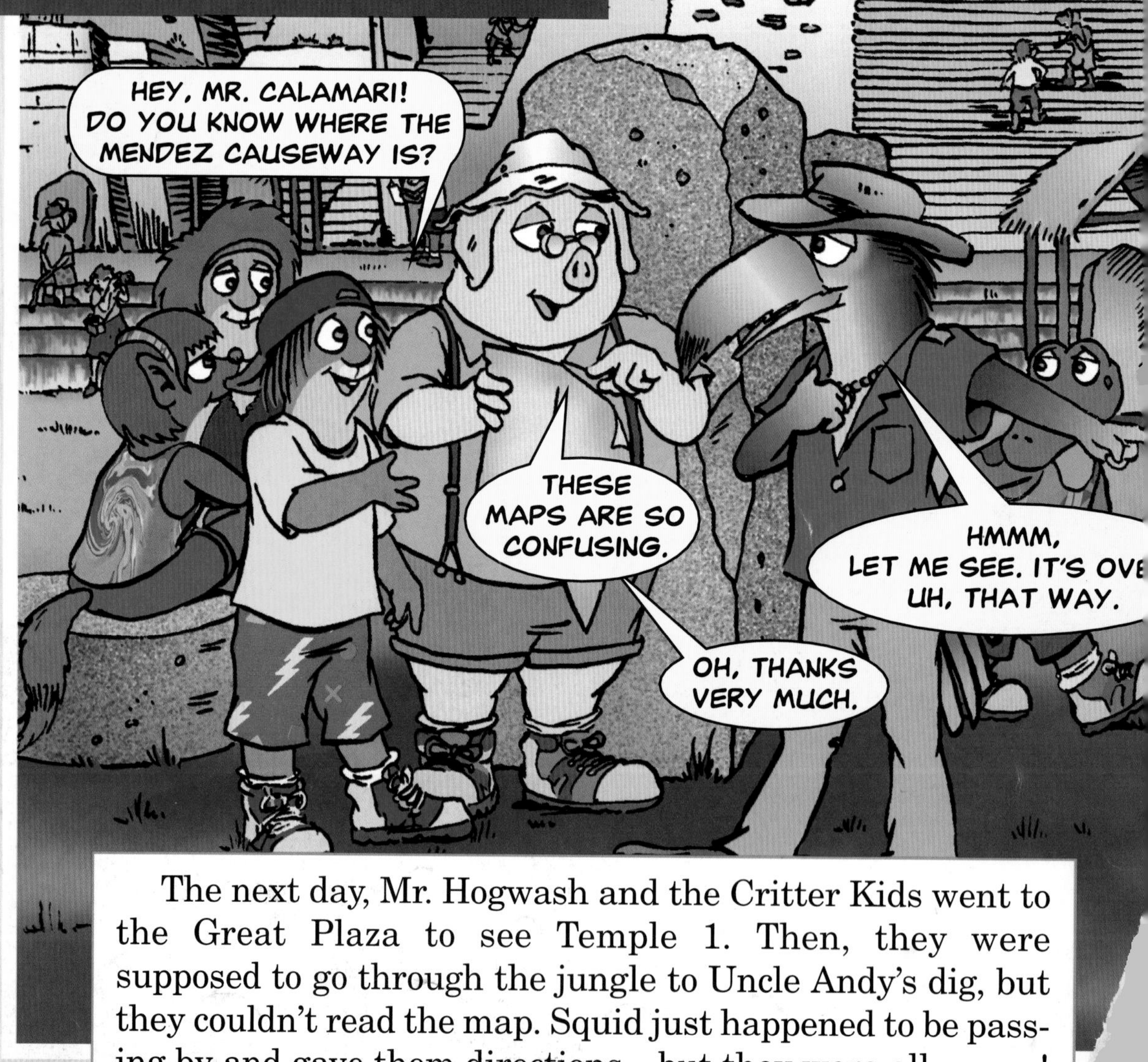
HEY, MR. CALAMARI! DO YOU KNOW WHERE THE MENDEZ CAUSEWAY IS?
THESE MAPS ARE SO CONFUSING.
HMMM, LET ME SEE. IT'S OVE UH, THAT WAY.
OH, THANKS VERY MUCH.

The next day, Mr. Hogwash and the Critter Kids went to the Great Plaza to see Temple 1. Then, they were supposed to go through the jungle to Uncle Andy's dig, but they couldn't read the map. Squid just happened to be passing by and gave them directions—but they were all wrong!

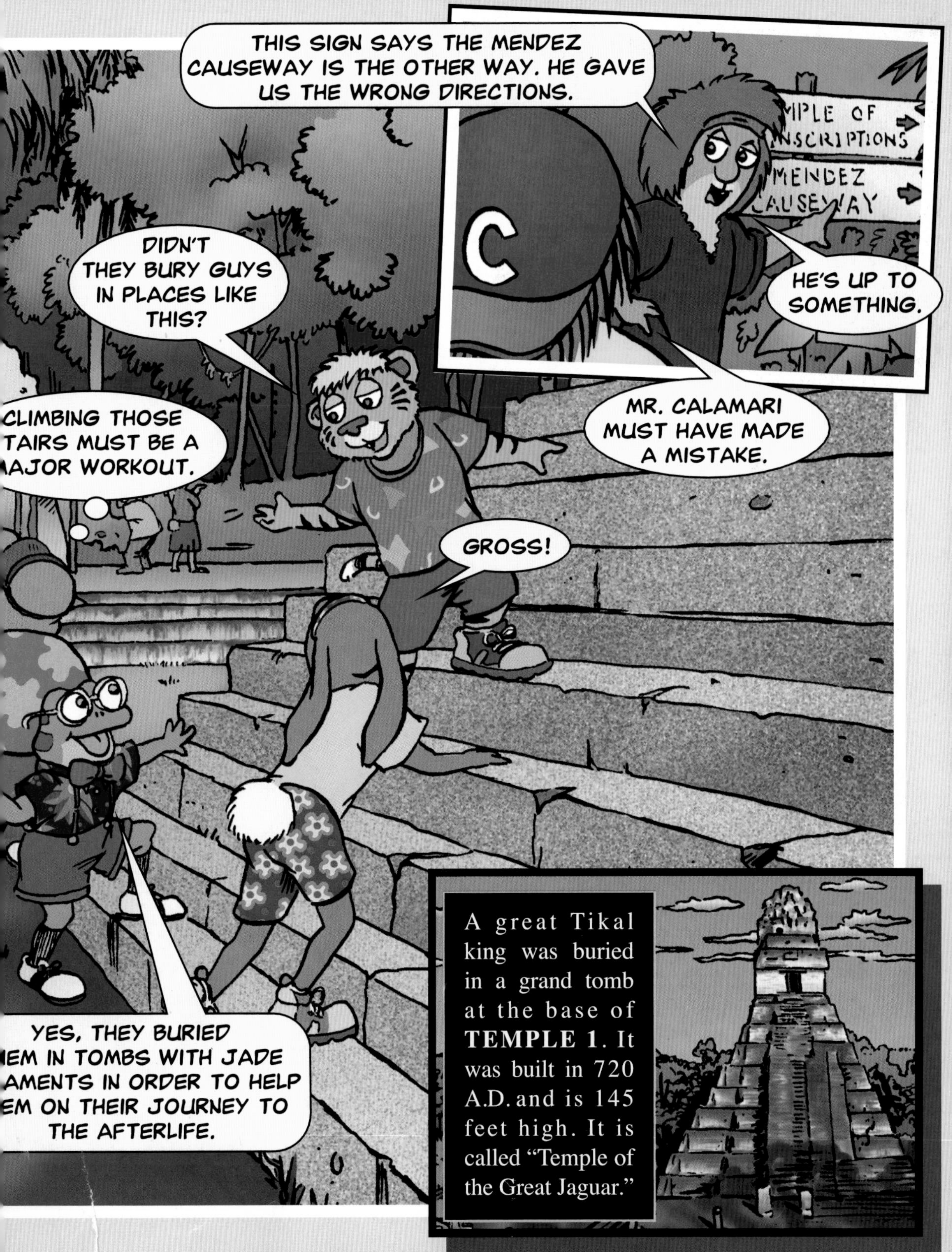
THIS SIGN SAYS THE MENDEZ CAUSEWAY IS THE OTHER WAY. HE GAVE US THE WRONG DIRECTIONS.
MPLE OF
NSCRIPTIONS
MENDEZ
AUSEWAY
HE'S UP TO SOMETHING.
MR. CALAMARI MUST HAVE MADE A MISTAKE.
DIDN'T THEY BURY GUYS IN PLACES LIKE THIS?
CLIMBING THOSE TAIRS MUST BE A AJOR WORKOUT.
GROSS!
YES, THEY BURIED IEM IN TOMBS WITH JADE AMENTS IN ORDER TO HELP EM ON THEIR JOURNEY TO THE AFTERLIFE.
A great Tikal king was buried in a grand tomb at the base of **TEMPLE 1**. It was built in 720 A.D. and is 145 feet high. It is called "Temple of the Great Jaguar."

STELAE are monuments carved out of stone that were made in honor of Maya rulers and important events. They were sometimes destroyed if a ruler died or was disgraced.

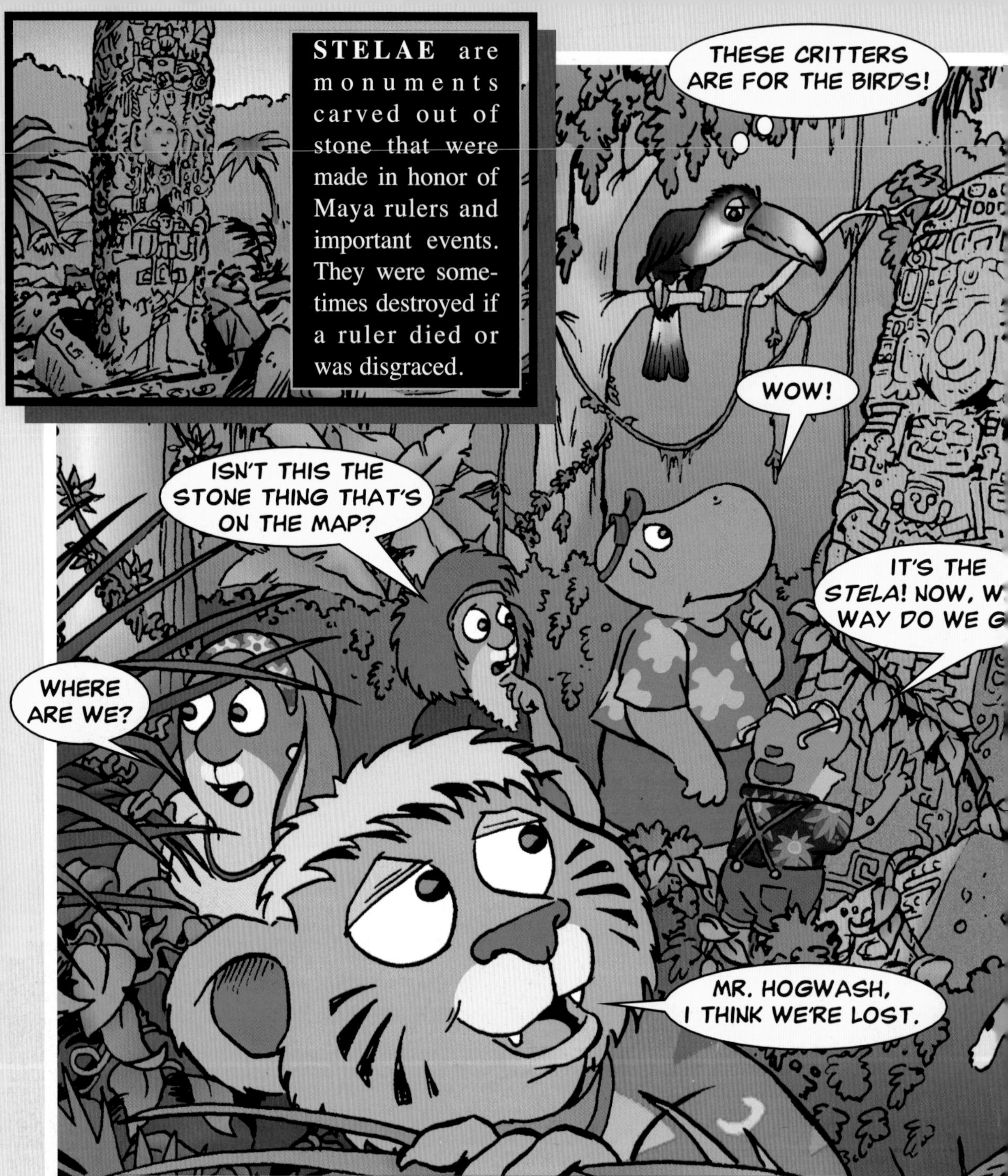
THESE CRITTERS ARE FOR THE BIRDS!
WOW!
ISN'T THIS THE STONE THING THAT'S ON THE MAP?
IT'S THE STELA! NOW, W
WAY DO WE G
WHERE ARE WE?
MR. HOGWASH, I THINK WE'RE LOST.

The Kids and Mr. Hogwash got lost in the jungle. Luckily, they met a friendly archaeologist, named Natasha, and her pet monkey, Kiki. Natasha gave them directions to Uncle Andy's dig.

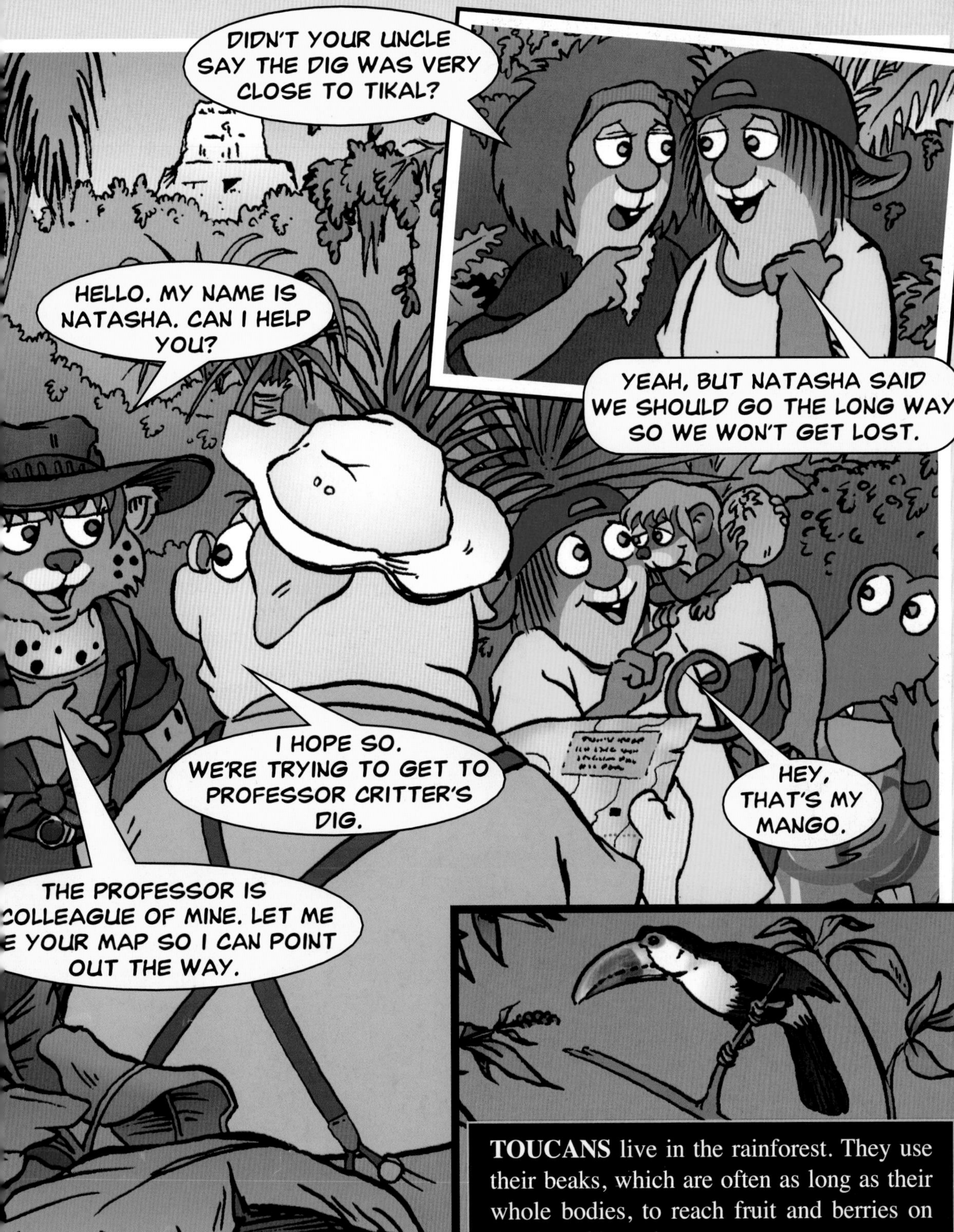
HELLO. MY NAME IS NATASHA. CAN I HELP YOU?
I HOPE SO. WE'RE TRYING TO GET TO PROFESSOR CRITTER'S DIG.
THE PROFESSOR IS COLLEAGUE OF MINE. LET ME E YOUR MAP SO I CAN POINT OUT THE WAY.
HEY, THAT'S MY MANGO.
DIDN'T YOUR UNCLE SAY THE DIG WAS VERY CLOSE TO TIKAL?
YEAH, BUT NATASHA SAID WE SHOULD GO THE LONG WAY SO WE WON'T GET LOST.

TOUCANS live in the rainforest. They use their beaks, which are often as long as their whole bodies, to reach fruit and berries on the tips of branches.

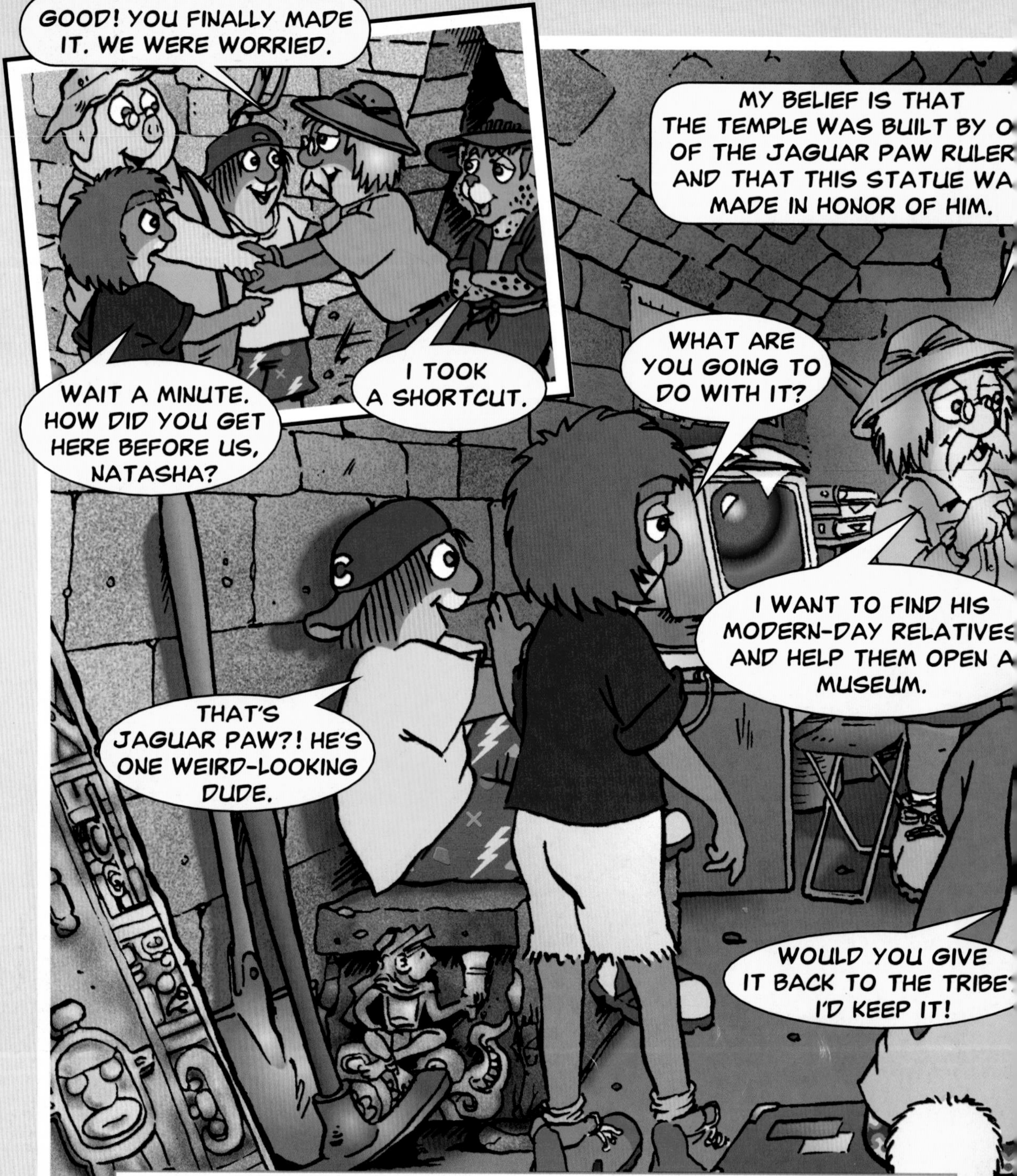
GOOD! YOU FINALLY MADE IT. WE WERE WORRIED.
WAIT A MINUTE. HOW DID YOU GET HERE BEFORE US, NATASHA?
I TOOK A SHORTCUT.
THAT'S JAGUAR PAW?! HE'S ONE WEIRD-LOOKING DUDE.
MY BELIEF IS THAT THE TEMPLE WAS BUILT BY O OF THE JAGUAR PAW RULER AND THAT THIS STATUE WA MADE IN HONOR OF HIM.
WHAT ARE YOU GOING TO DO WITH IT?
I WANT TO FIND HIS MODERN-DAY RELATIVES AND HELP THEM OPEN A MUSEUM.
WOULD YOU GIVE IT BACK TO THE TRIBE I'D KEEP IT!

Mr. Hogwash and the Critter Kids followed Natasha's directions, but somehow they got lost again. When they finally made it to the dig, Natasha was already there. After she left, Uncle Andy showed them the Jaguar Paw statue.

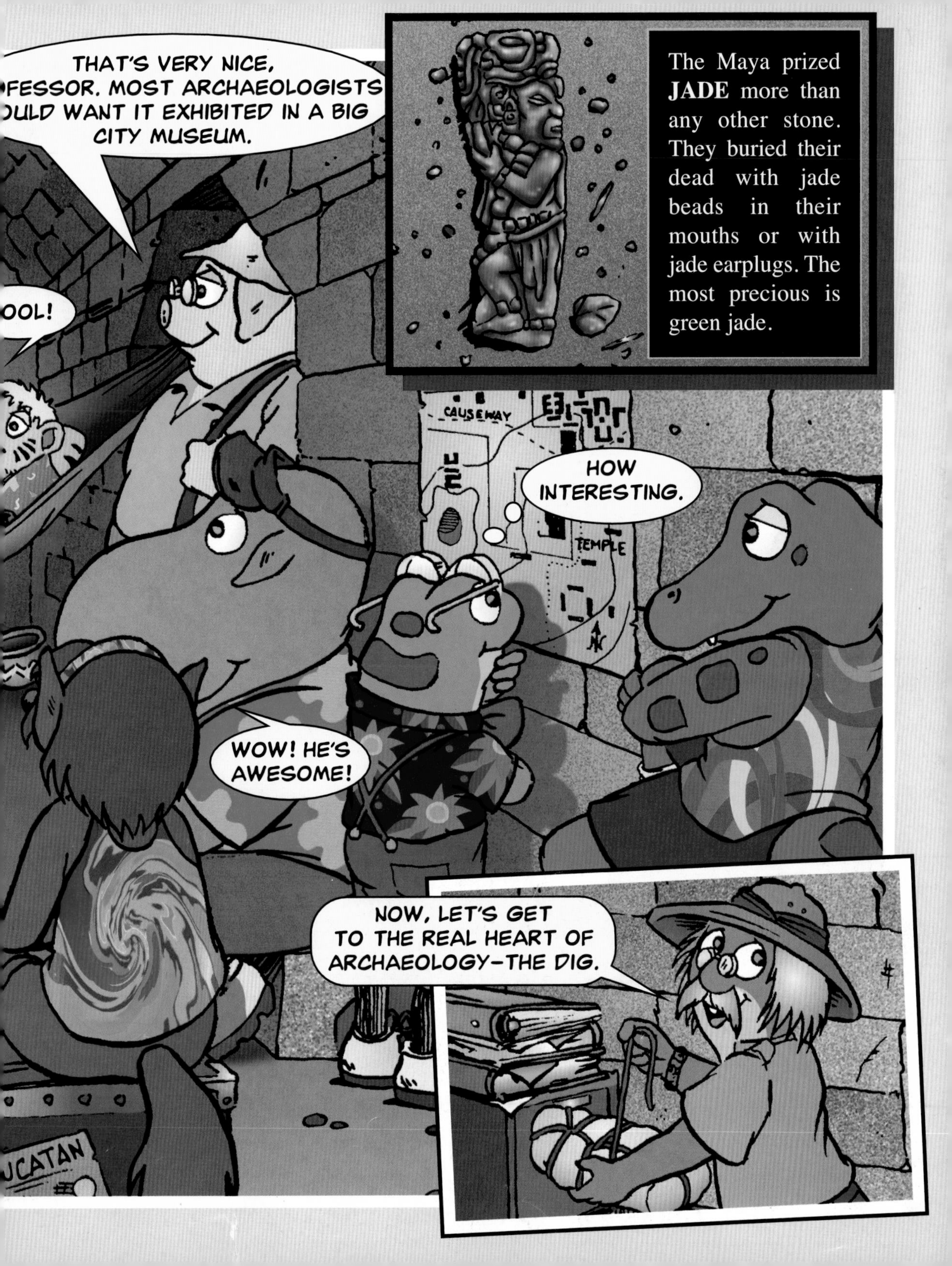
THAT'S VERY NICE, FESSOR. MOST ARCHAEOLOGISTS ULD WANT IT EXHIBITED IN A BIG CITY MUSEUM.
OOL!
The Maya prized **JADE** more than any other stone. They buried their dead with jade beads in their mouths or with jade earplugs. The most precious is green jade.
CAUSEWAY
TEMPLE
HOW INTERESTING.
WOW! HE'S AWESOME!
NOW, LET'S GET TO THE REAL HEART OF ARCHAEOLOGY–THE DIG.
UCATAN

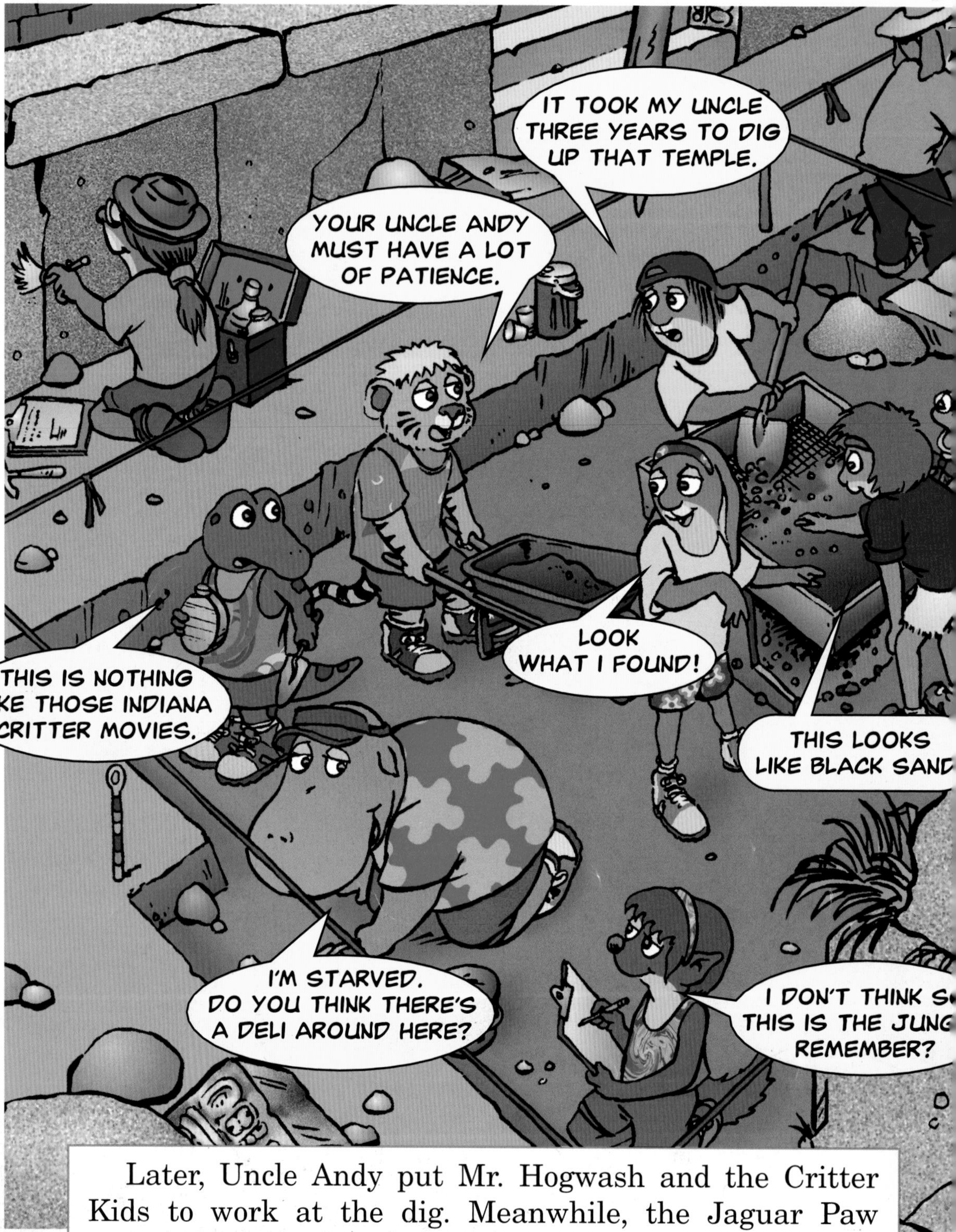

IT TOOK MY UNCLE THREE YEARS TO DIG UP THAT TEMPLE.
YOUR UNCLE ANDY MUST HAVE A LOT OF PATIENCE.
THIS IS NOTHING LIKE THOSE INDIANA CRITTER MOVIES.
LOOK WHAT I FOUND!
THIS LOOKS LIKE BLACK SAND
I'M STARVED. DO YOU THINK THERE'S A DELI AROUND HERE?
I DON'T THINK S
THIS IS THE JUNG
REMEMBER?

Later, Uncle Andy put Mr. Hogwash and the Critter Kids to work at the dig. Meanwhile, the Jaguar Paw statue disappeared!

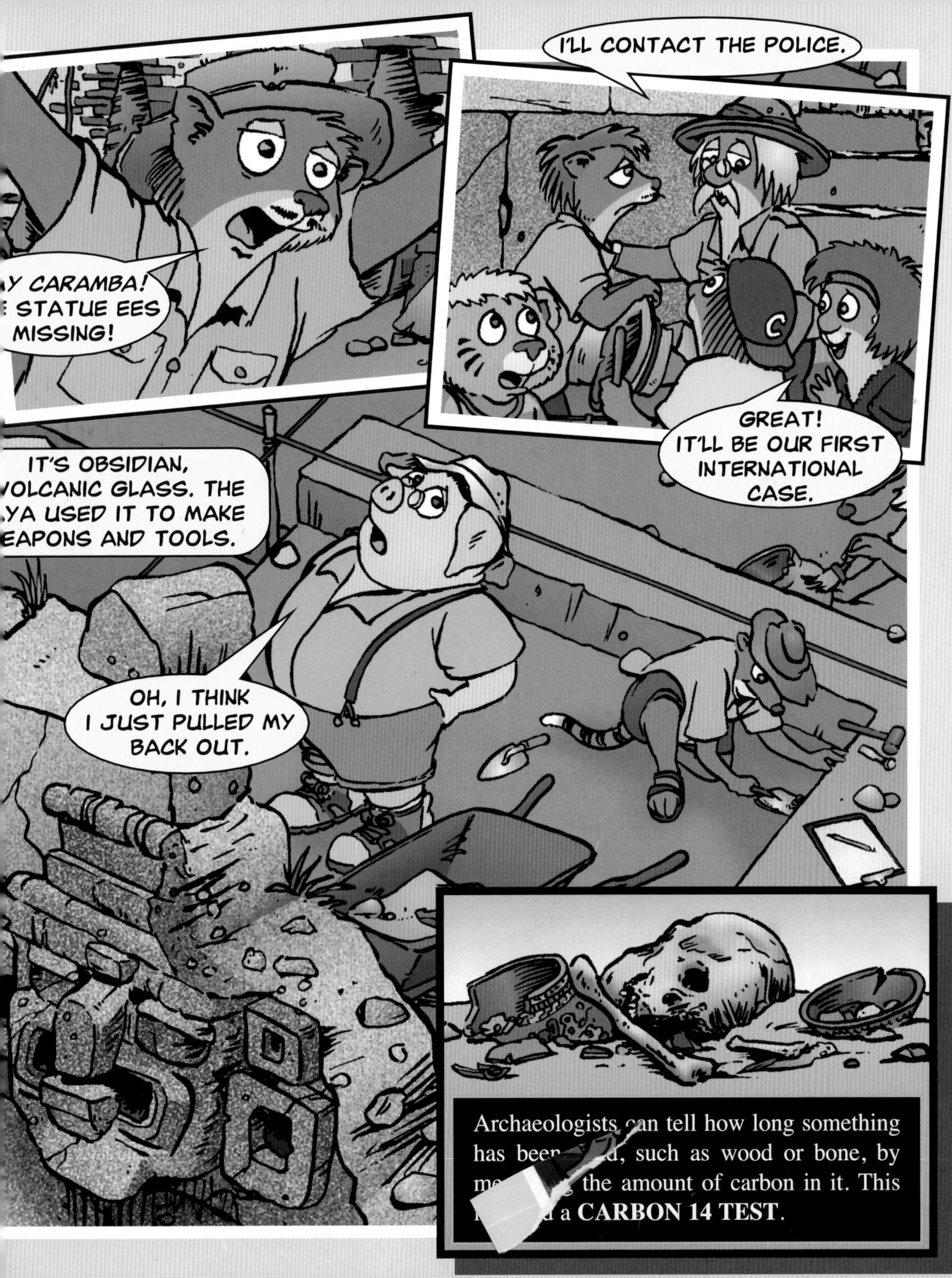
Y CARAMBA! STATUE EES MISSING!
I'LL CONTACT THE POLICE.
GREAT! IT'LL BE OUR FIRST INTERNATIONAL CASE.
IT'S OBSIDIAN, OLCANIC GLASS. THE YA USED IT TO MAKE EAPONS AND TOOLS.
OH, I THINK I JUST PULLED MY BACK OUT.
Archaeologists can tell how long something has been d, such as wood or bone, by me the amount of carbon in it. This a **CARBON 14 TEST**.

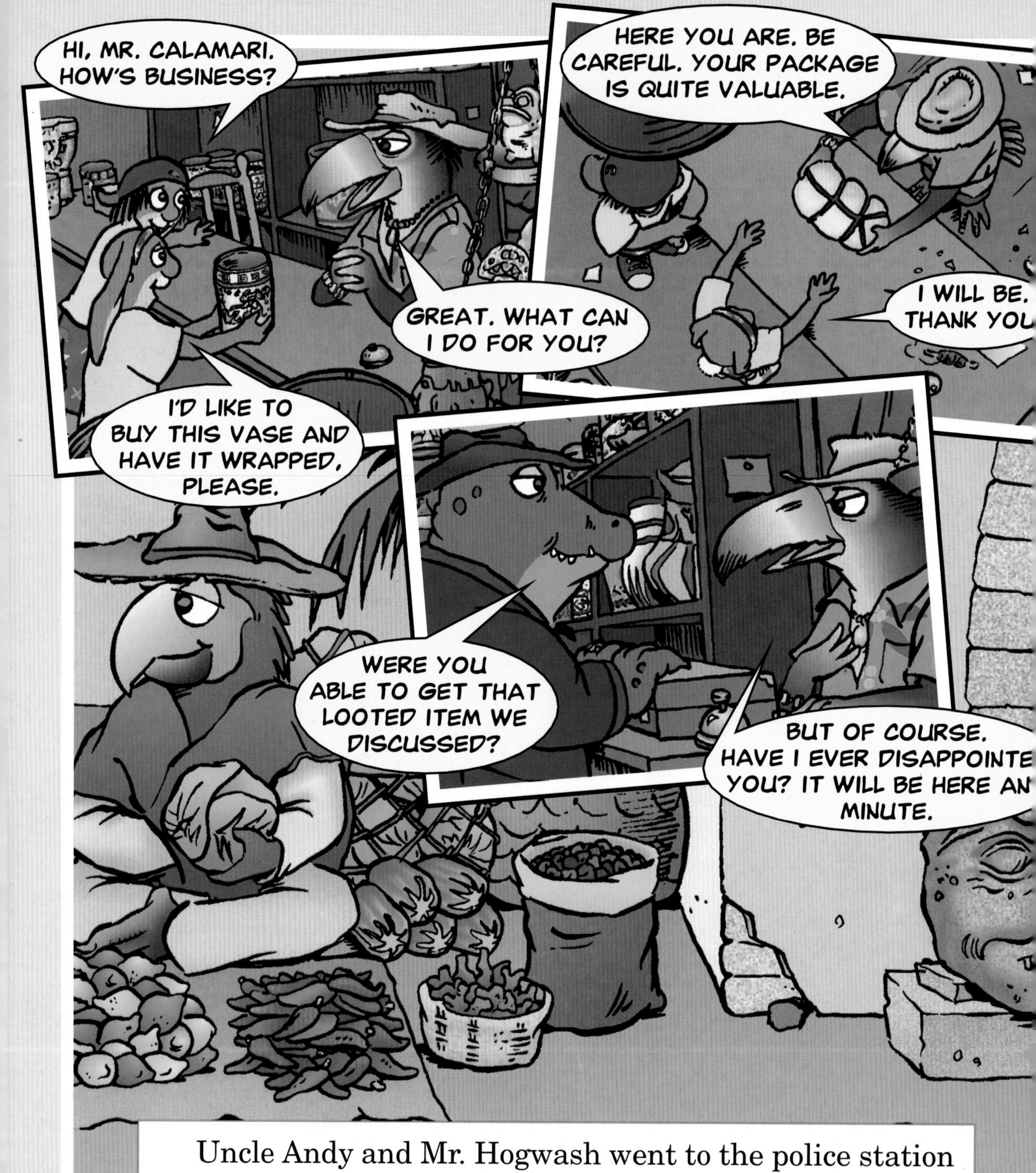
HI, MR. CALAMARI. HOW'S BUSINESS?
GREAT. WHAT CAN I DO FOR YOU?
I'D LIKE TO BUY THIS VASE AND HAVE IT WRAPPED, PLEASE.
HERE YOU ARE. BE CAREFUL. YOUR PACKAGE IS QUITE VALUABLE.
I WILL BE. THANK YOU
WERE YOU ABLE TO GET THAT LOOTED ITEM WE DISCUSSED?
BUT OF COURSE. HAVE I EVER DISAPPOINTE YOU? IT WILL BE HERE AN MINUTE.

Uncle Andy and Mr. Hogwash went to the police station to report the theft of the Jaguar Paw statue, while the Kids went to Maya Mundo to buy some souvenirs. When they were leaving the store, a strange critter bumped into Su Su, and they both dropped their packages.

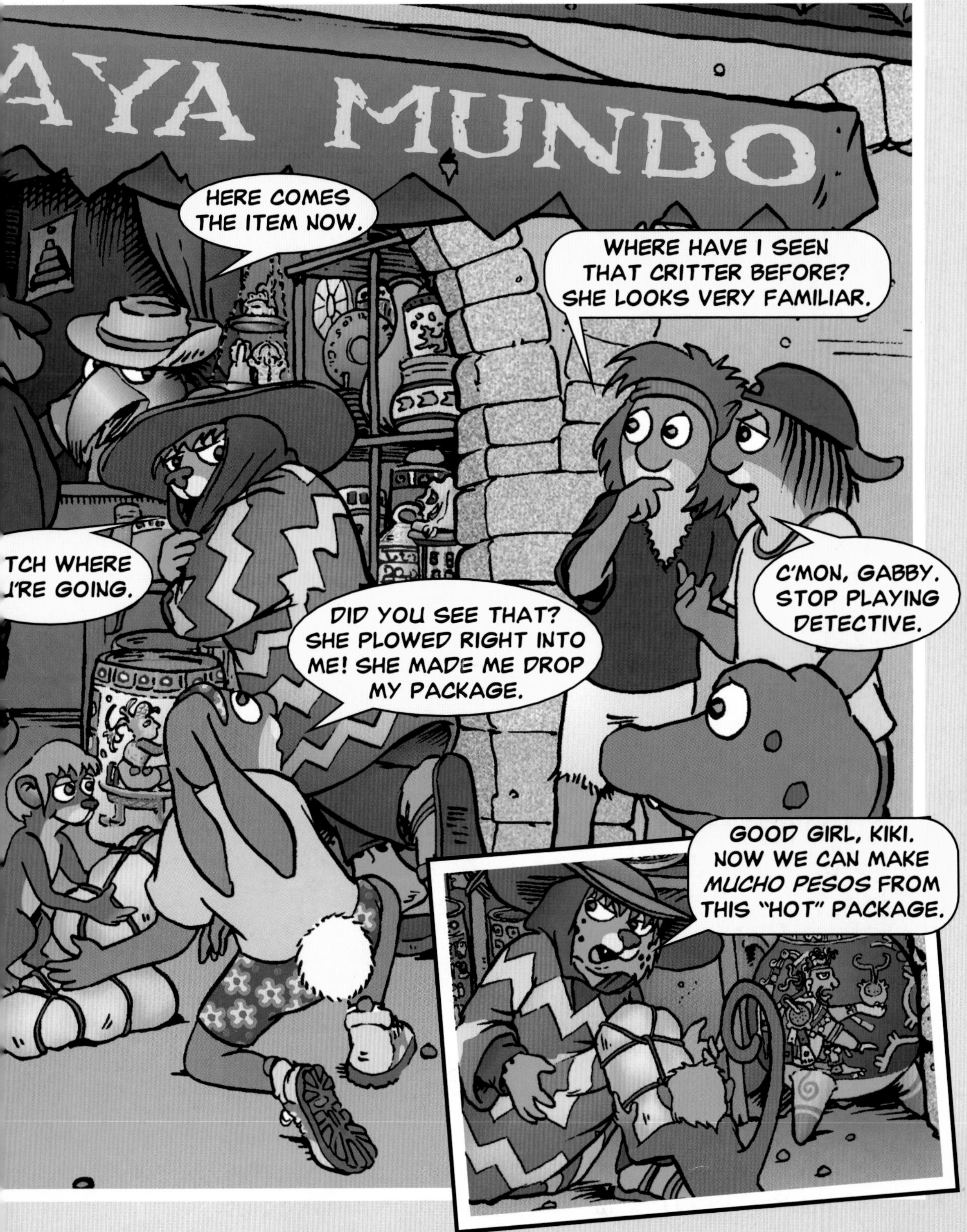
AYA MUNDO
HERE COMES THE ITEM NOW.
TCH WHERE
'RE GOING.
WHERE HAVE I SEEN THAT CRITTER BEFORE? SHE LOOKS VERY FAMILIAR.
C'MON, GABBY. STOP PLAYING DETECTIVE.
DID YOU SEE THAT? SHE PLOWED RIGHT INTO ME! SHE MADE ME DROP MY PACKAGE.
GOOD GIRL, KIKI. NOW WE CAN MAKE *MUCHO PESOS* FROM THIS "HOT" PACKAGE.

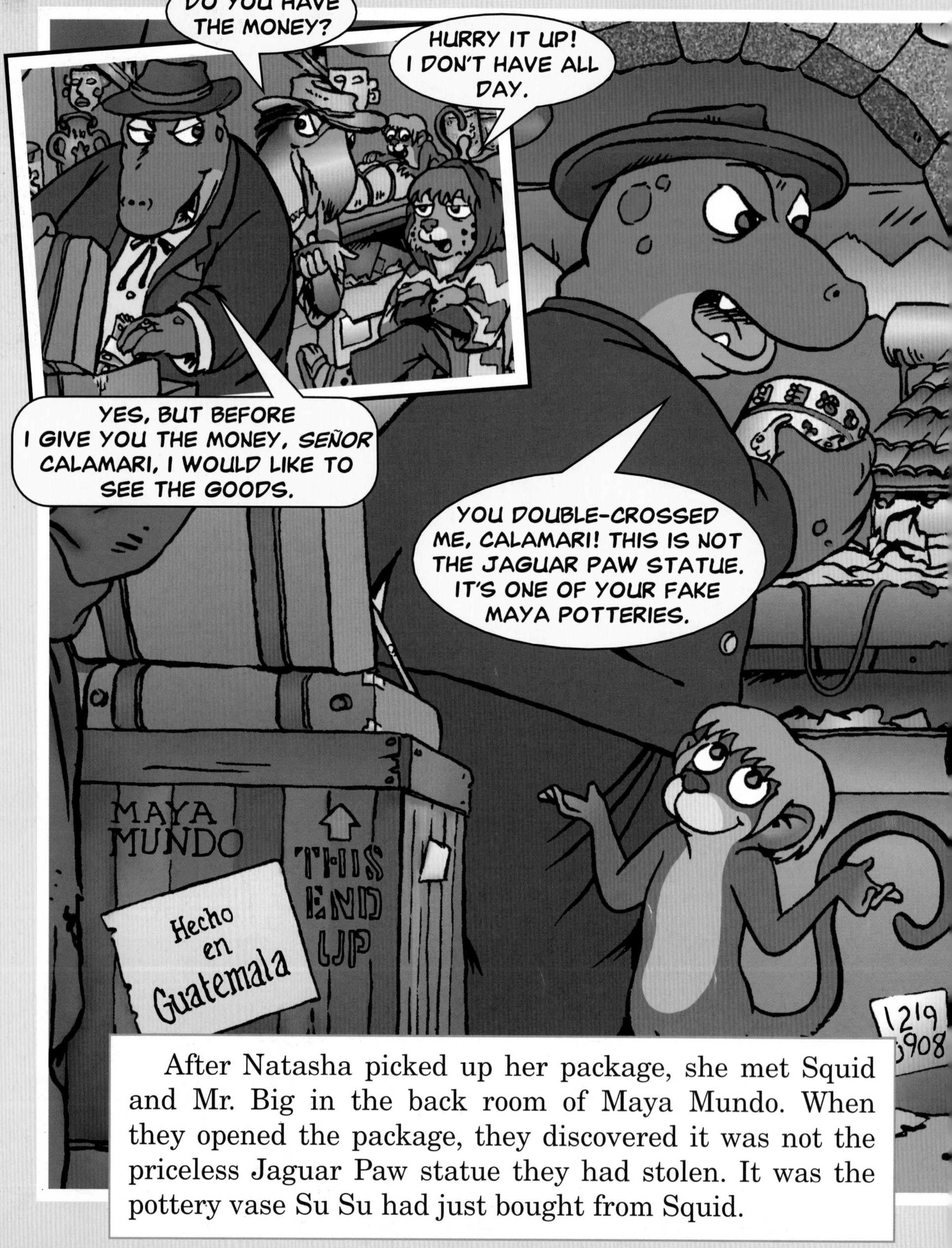
DO YOU HAVE THE MONEY?
HURRY IT UP! I DON'T HAVE ALL DAY.
YES, BUT BEFORE I GIVE YOU THE MONEY, *SEÑOR* CALAMARI, I WOULD LIKE TO SEE THE GOODS.
YOU DOUBLE-CROSSED ME, CALAMARI! THIS IS NOT THE JAGUAR PAW STATUE. IT'S ONE OF YOUR FAKE MAYA POTTERIES.
MAYA MUNDO
THIS END UP
Hecho en Guatemala

After Natasha picked up her package, she met Squid and Mr. Big in the back room of Maya Mundo. When they opened the package, they discovered it was not the priceless Jaguar Paw statue they had stolen. It was the pottery vase Su Su had just bought from Squid.

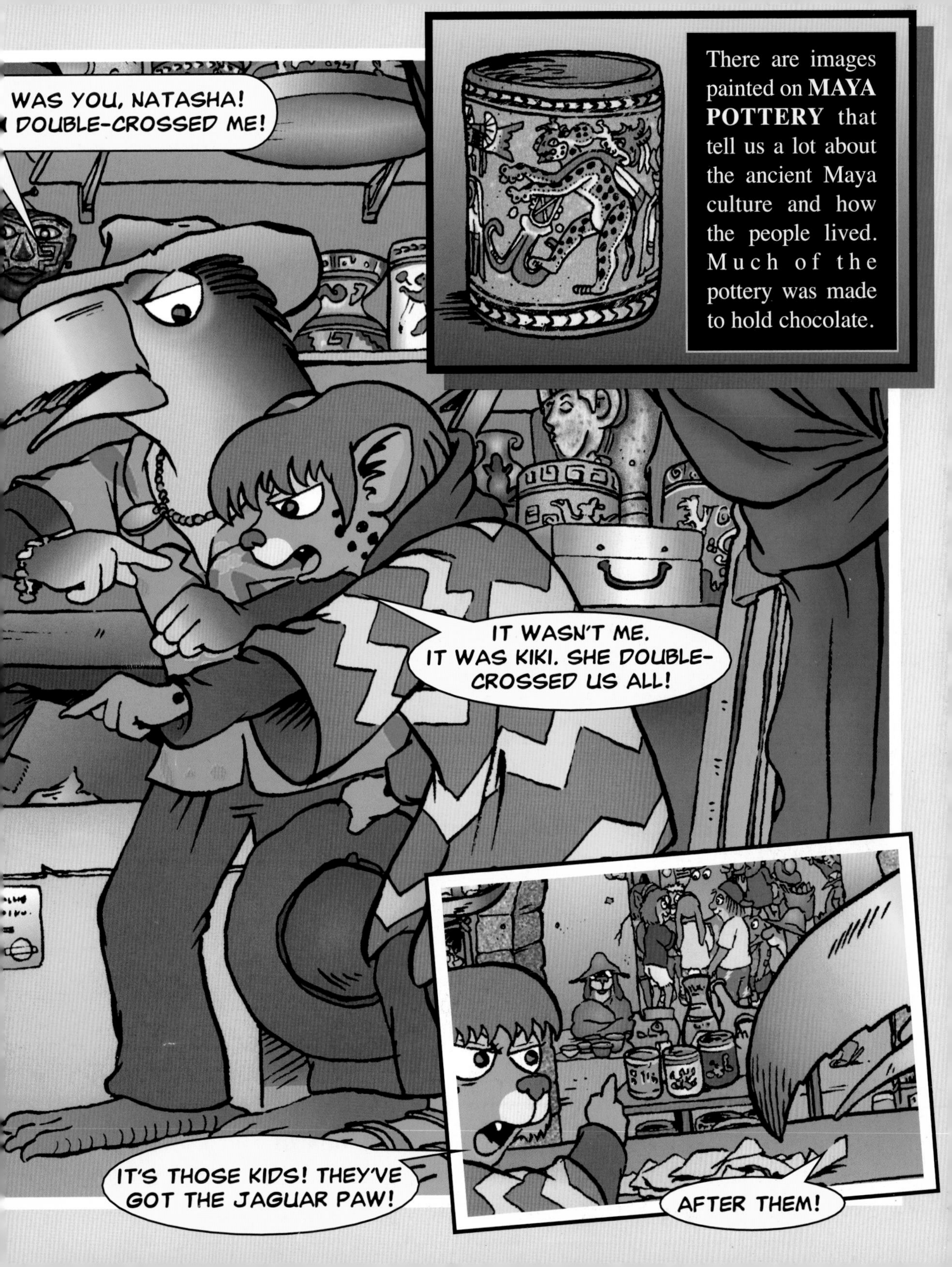

WAS YOU, NATASHA! DOUBLE-CROSSED ME!
There are images painted on **MAYA POTTERY** that tell us a lot about the ancient Maya culture and how the people lived. Much of the pottery was made to hold chocolate.
IT WASN'T ME. IT WAS KIKI. SHE DOUBLE-CROSSED US ALL!
IT'S THOSE KIDS! THEY'VE GOT THE JAGUAR PAW!
AFTER THEM!

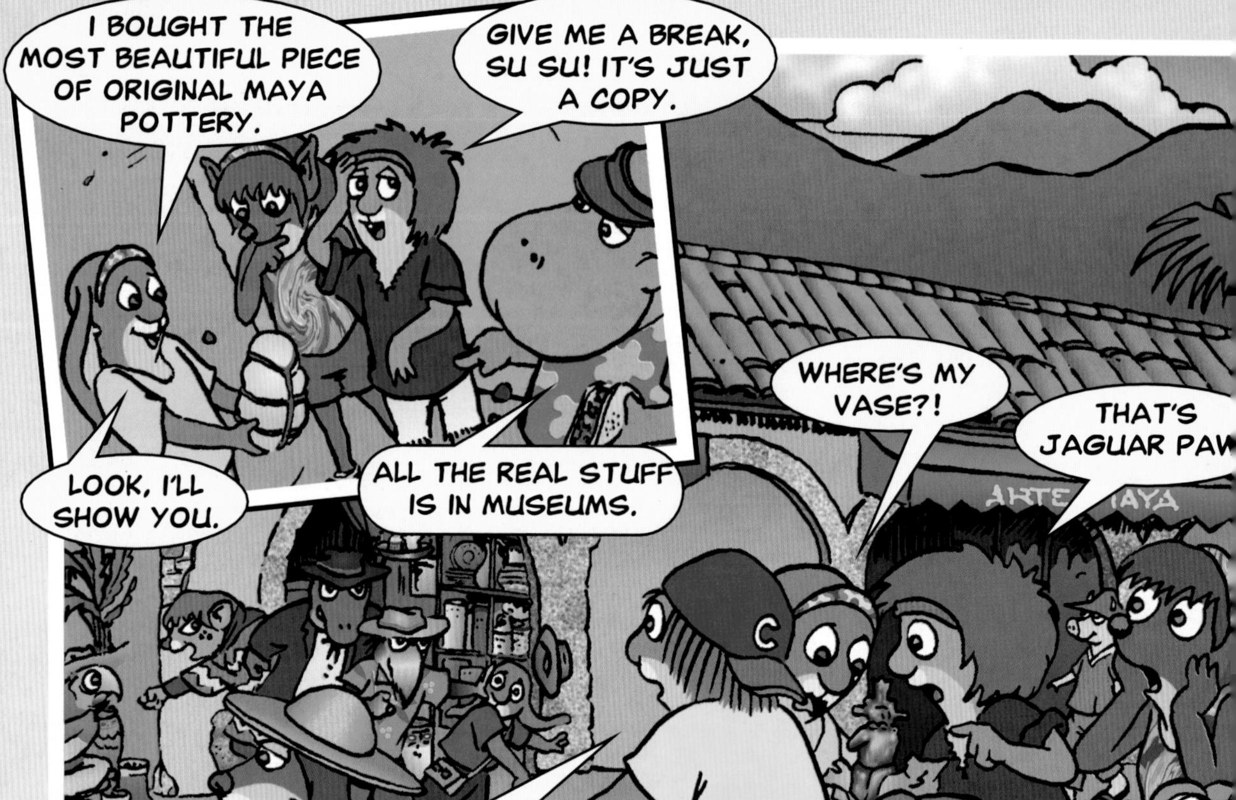

I BOUGHT THE MOST BEAUTIFUL PIECE OF ORIGINAL MAYA POTTERY.
GIVE ME A BREAK, SU SU! IT'S JUST A COPY.
LOOK, I'LL SHOW YOU.
ALL THE REAL STUFF IS IN MUSEUMS.
WHERE'S MY VASE?!
THAT'S JAGUAR PAW
LOOK WHO'S COMING! THEY MUST HAVE STOLEN IT.
WHAT ARE WE GONNA DO?
WE BETTER GET ON THE BUS.

Outside the store, Su Su unwrapped her package to show everyone what she had bought. Everyone gasped! It wasn't her vase—it was the Jaguar Paw statue! Just then, Squid, Mr. Big, and Natasha burst out of the store. The Kids had to make a quick getaway, so they hopped on a bus that was headed for the jungle.

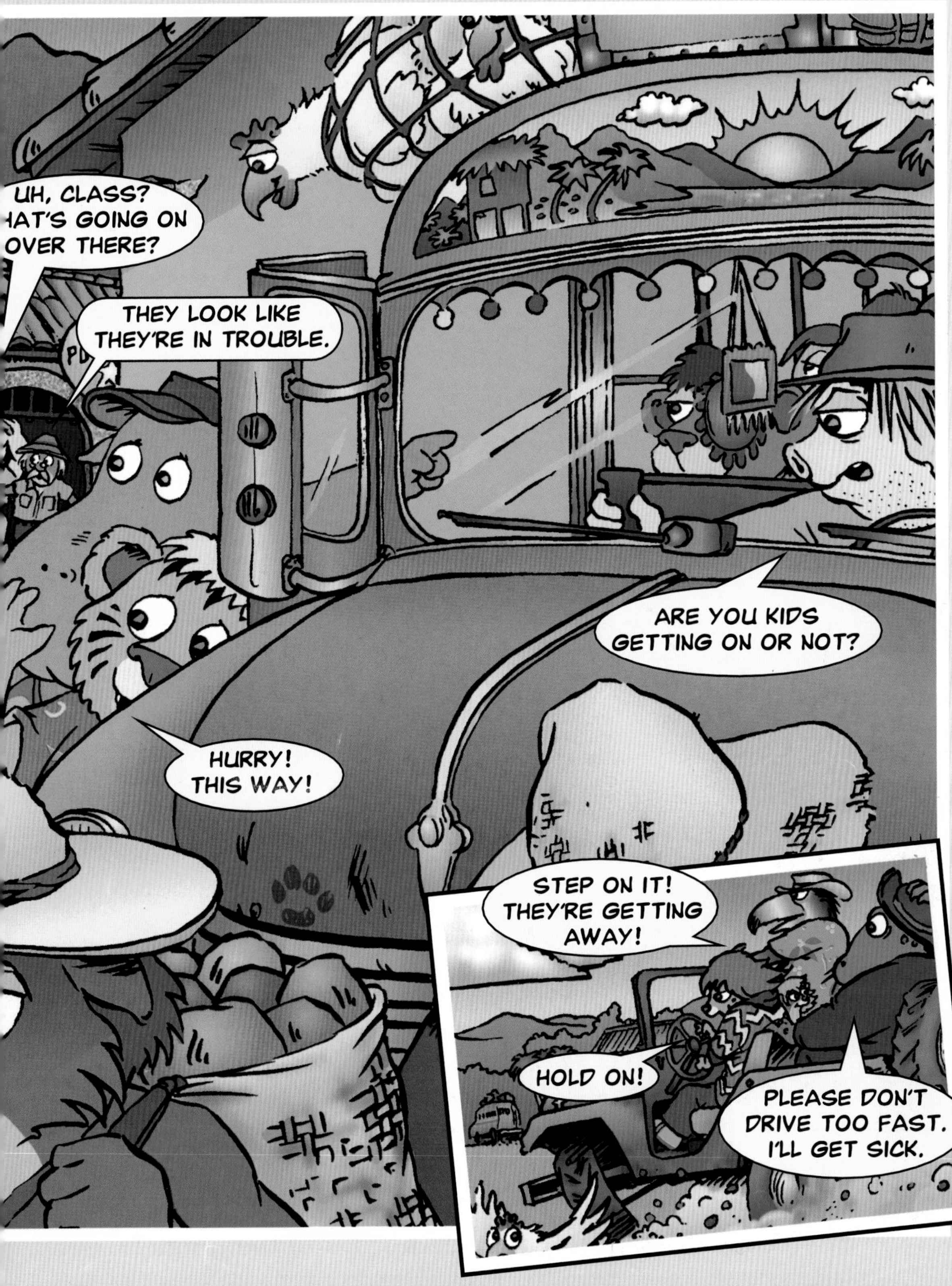
UH, CLASS? HAT'S GOING ON OVER THERE?
THEY LOOK LIKE THEY'RE IN TROUBLE.
ARE YOU KIDS GETTING ON OR NOT?
HURRY! THIS WAY!
STEP ON IT! THEY'RE GETTING AWAY!
HOLD ON!
PLEASE DON'T DRIVE TOO FAST. I'LL GET SICK.

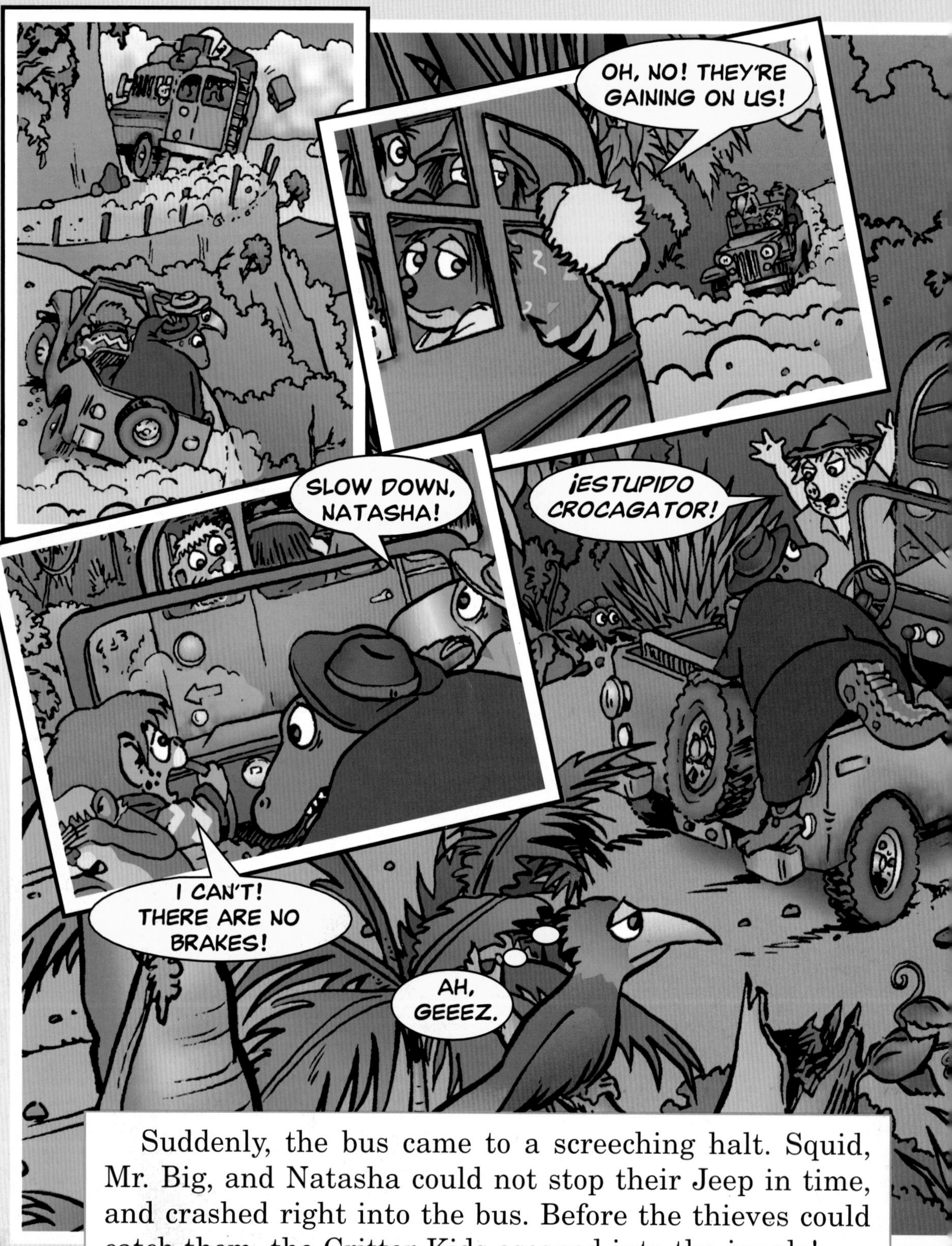
OH, NO! THEY'RE GAINING ON US!
SLOW DOWN, NATASHA!
¡ESTUPIDO CROCAGATOR!
I CAN'T! THERE ARE NO BRAKES!
AH, GEEEZ.

Suddenly, the bus came to a screeching halt. Squid, Mr. Big, and Natasha could not stop their Jeep in time, and crashed right into the bus. Before the thieves could catch them, the Critter Kids escaped into the jungle!

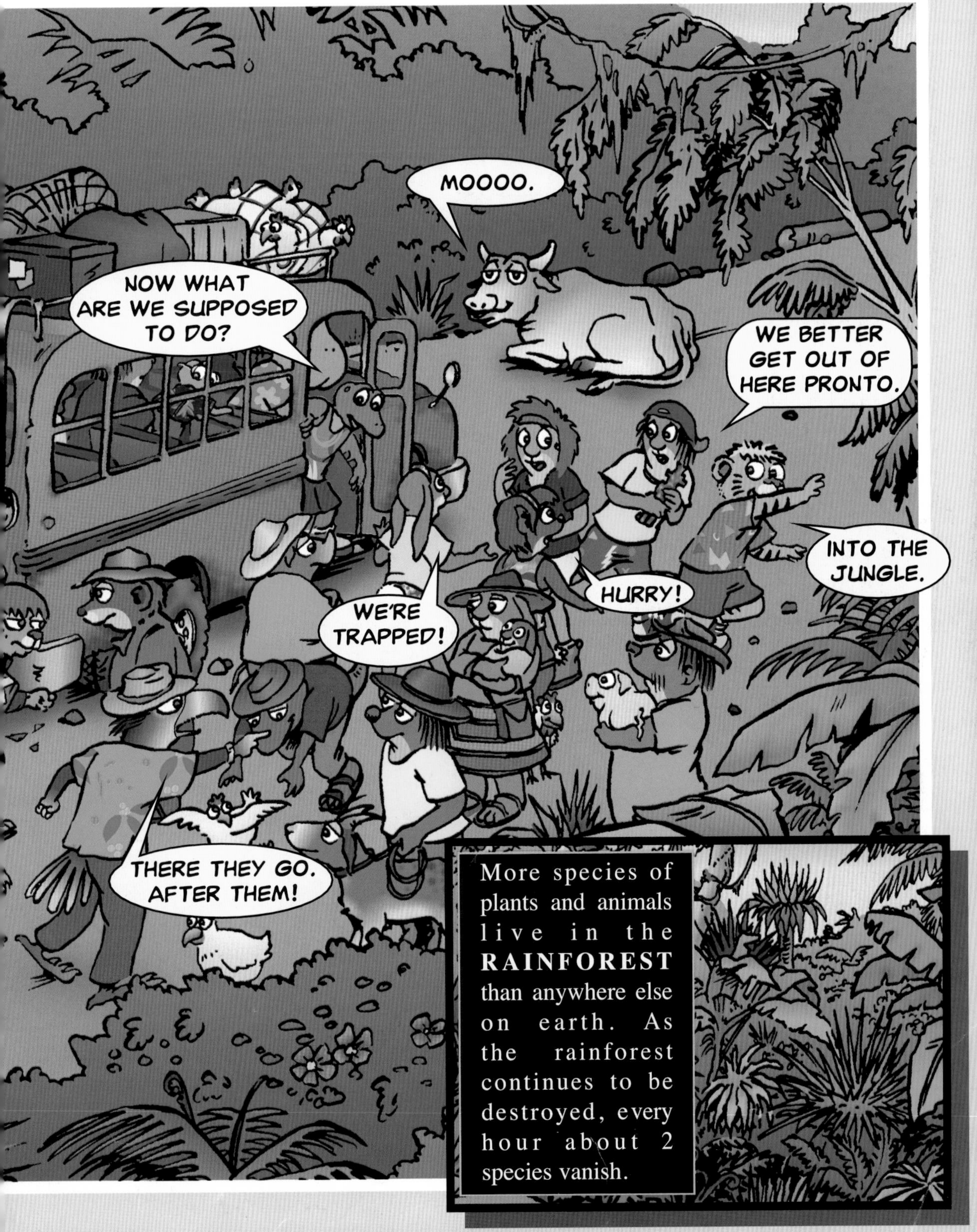
MOOOO.
NOW WHAT ARE WE SUPPOSED TO DO?
WE BETTER GET OUT OF HERE PRONTO.
WE'RE TRAPPED!
HURRY!
INTO THE JUNGLE.
THERE THEY GO. AFTER THEM!

More species of plants and animals live in the **RAINFOREST** than anywhere else on earth. As the rainforest continues to be destroyed, every hour about 2 species vanish.

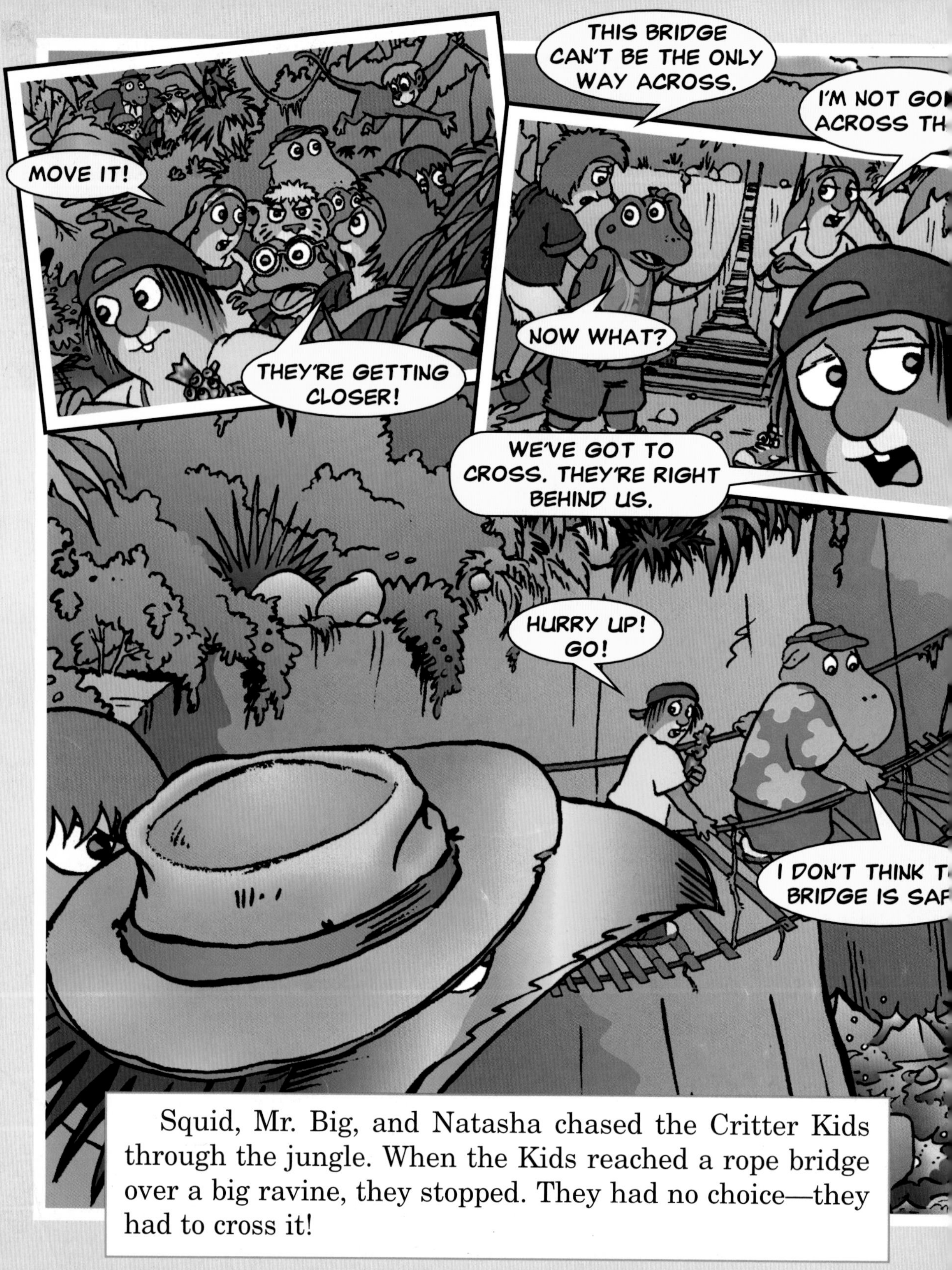
MOVE IT!
THEY'RE GETTING CLOSER!
THIS BRIDGE CAN'T BE THE ONLY WAY ACROSS.
NOW WHAT?
I'M NOT GO ACROSS TH
WE'VE GOT TO CROSS. THEY'RE RIGHT BEHIND US.
HURRY UP! GO!
I DON'T THINK T BRIDGE IS SAF

Squid, Mr. Big, and Natasha chased the Critter Kids through the jungle. When the Kids reached a rope bridge over a big ravine, they stopped. They had no choice—they had to cross it!

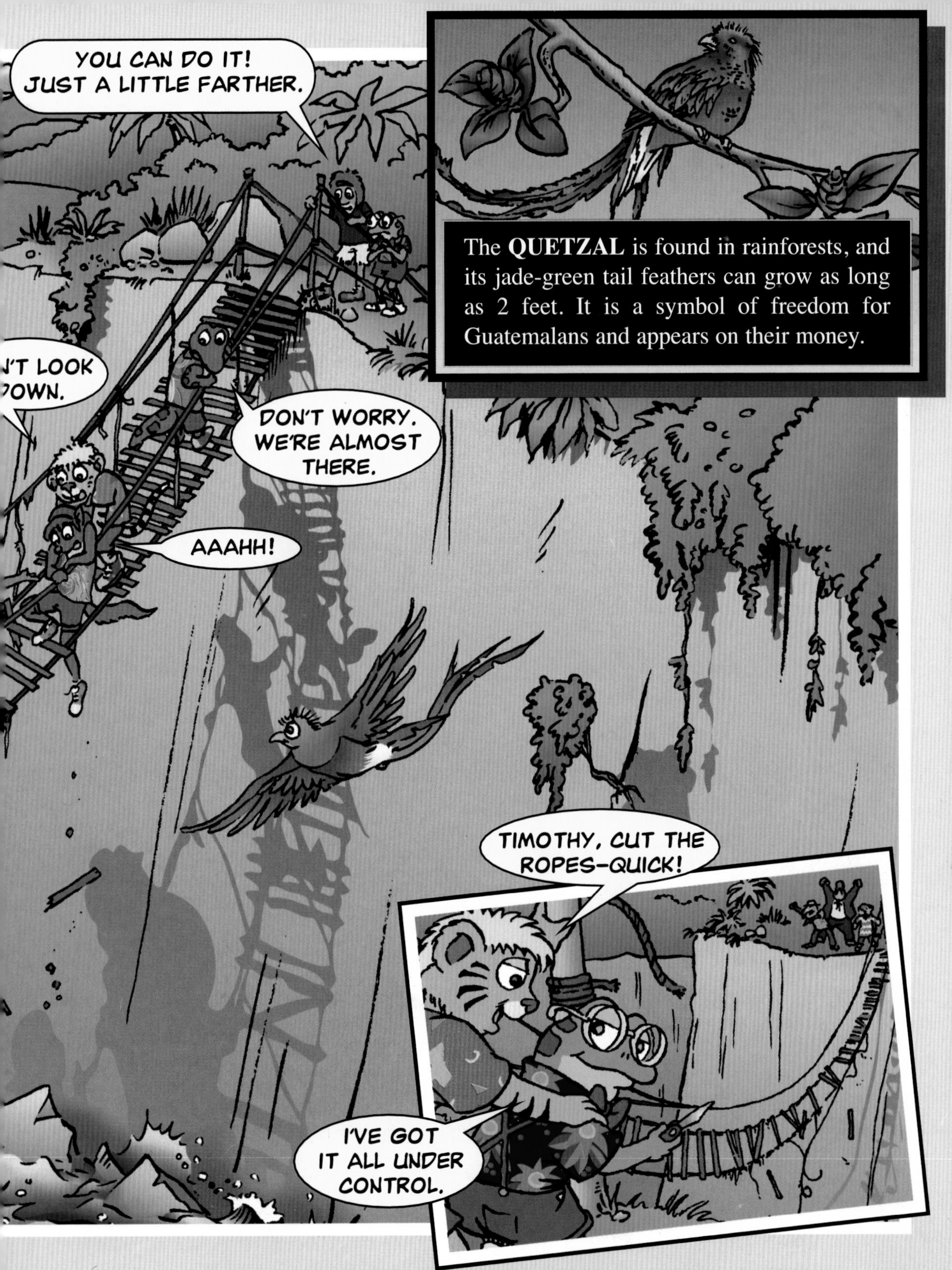
YOU CAN DO IT! JUST A LITTLE FARTHER.
The **QUETZAL** is found in rainforests, and its jade-green tail feathers can grow as long as 2 feet. It is a symbol of freedom for Guatemalans and appears on their money.
'T LOOK DOWN.
DON'T WORRY. WE'RE ALMOST THERE.
AAAHH!
TIMOTHY, CUT THE ROPES–QUICK!
I'VE GOT IT ALL UNDER CONTROL.

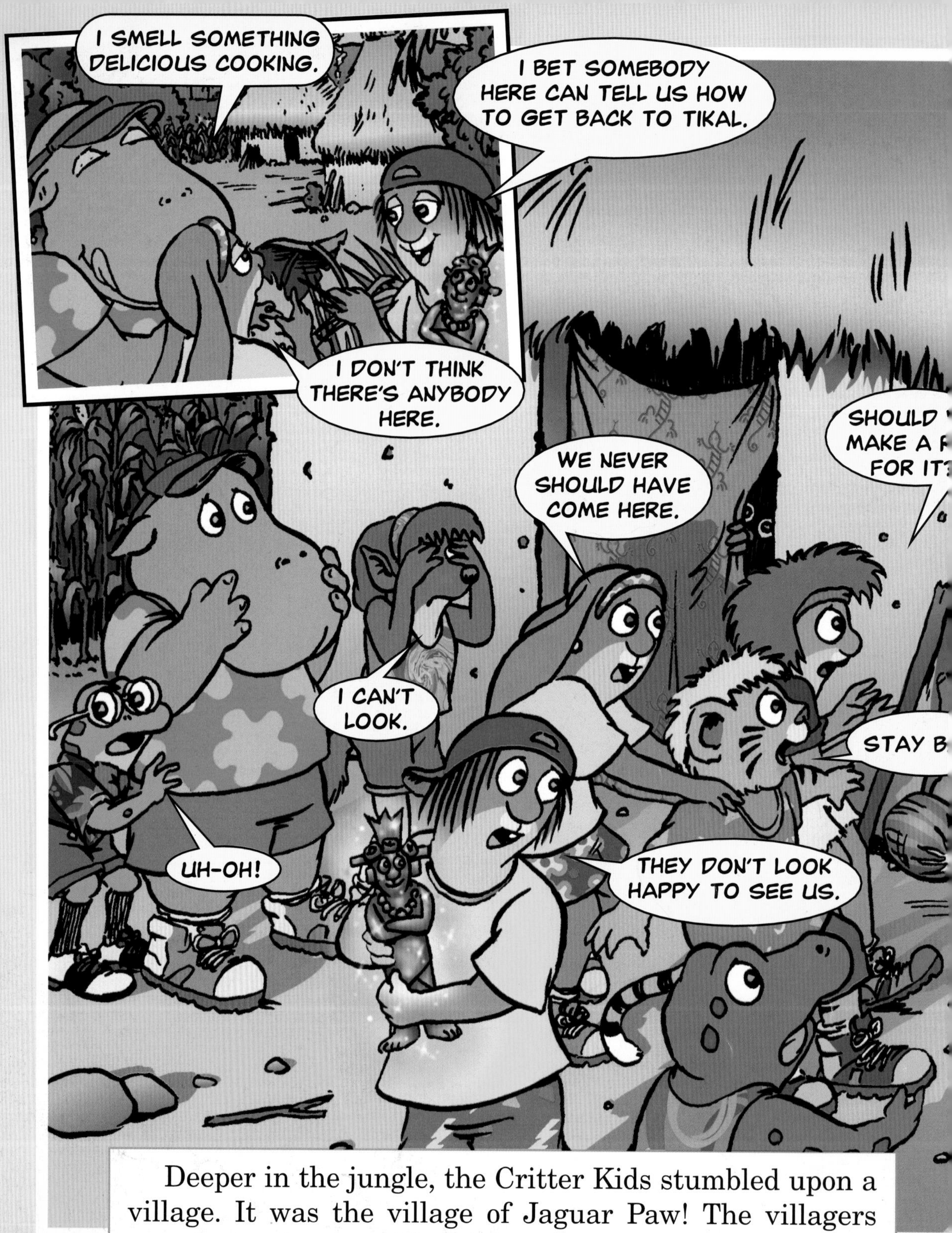
I SMELL SOMETHING DELICIOUS COOKING.
I BET SOMEBODY HERE CAN TELL US HOW TO GET BACK TO TIKAL.
I DON'T THINK THERE'S ANYBODY HERE.
WE NEVER SHOULD HAVE COME HERE.
SHOULD
MAKE A
FOR IT
I CAN'T LOOK.
STAY
UH-OH!
THEY DON'T LOOK HAPPY TO SEE US.

Deeper in the jungle, the Critter Kids stumbled upon a village. It was the village of Jaguar Paw! The villagers were preparing for a big fiesta and invited the Kids to stay.

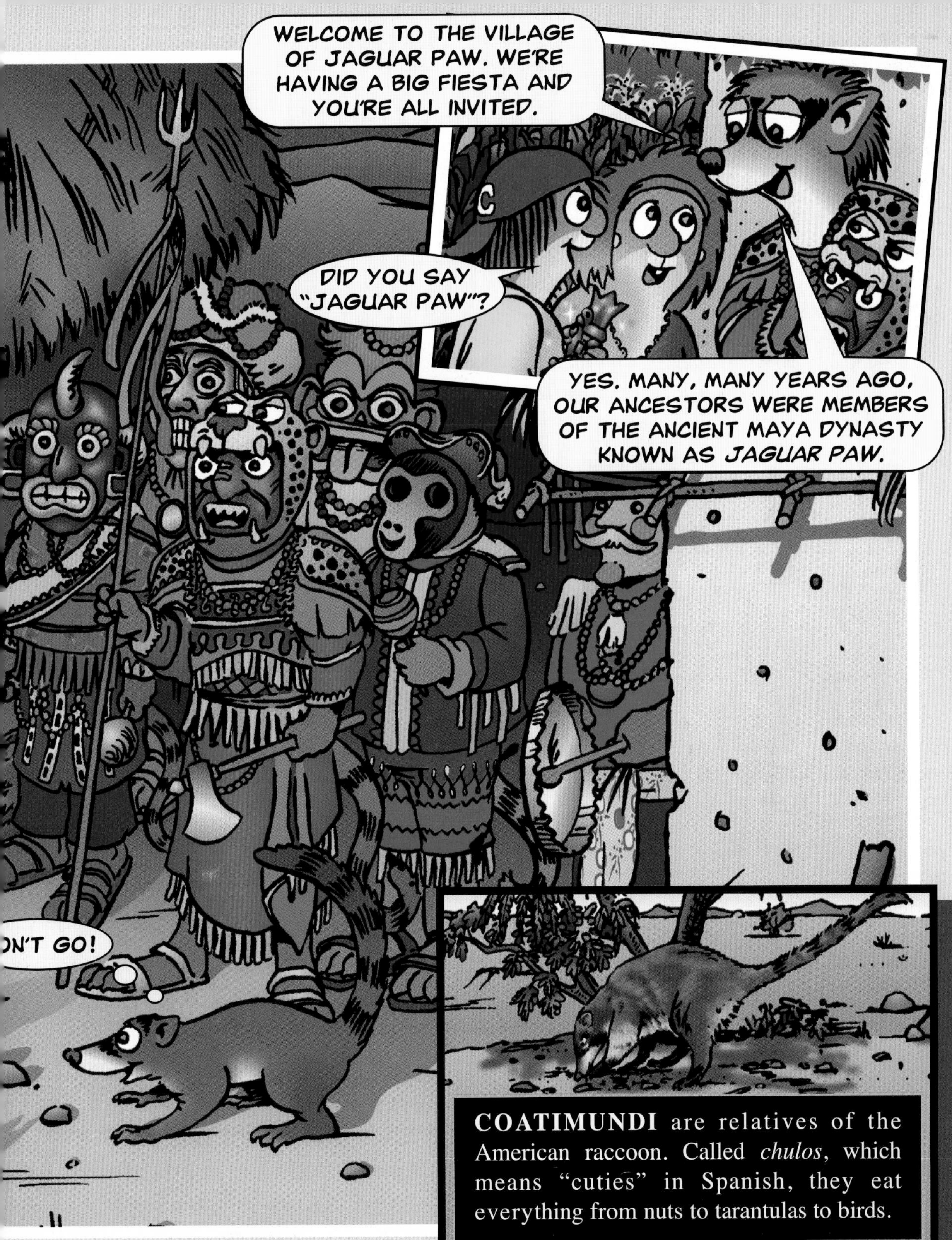
WELCOME TO THE VILLAGE OF JAGUAR PAW. WE'RE HAVING A BIG FIESTA AND YOU'RE ALL INVITED.
DID YOU SAY "JAGUAR PAW"?
YES. MANY, MANY YEARS AGO, OUR ANCESTORS WERE MEMBERS OF THE ANCIENT MAYA DYNASTY KNOWN AS *JAGUAR PAW.*
...N'T GO!

COATIMUNDI are relatives of the American raccoon. Called *chulos*, which means "cuties" in Spanish, they eat everything from nuts to tarantulas to birds.

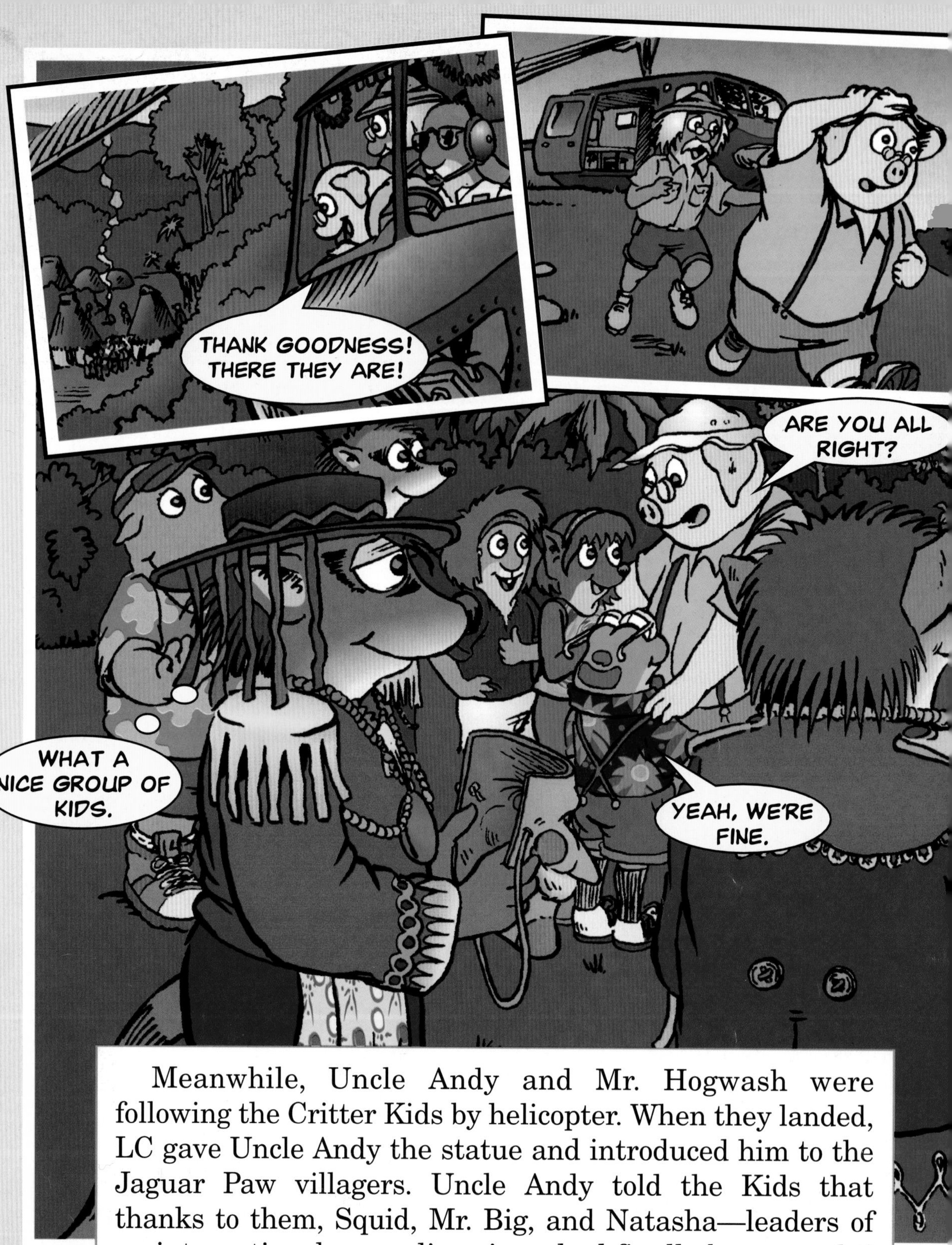
THANK GOODNESS! THERE THEY ARE!
ARE YOU ALL RIGHT?
WHAT A NICE GROUP OF KIDS.
YEAH, WE'RE FINE.

Meanwhile, Uncle Andy and Mr. Hogwash were following the Critter Kids by helicopter. When they landed, LC gave Uncle Andy the statue and introduced him to the Jaguar Paw villagers. Uncle Andy told the Kids that thanks to them, Squid, Mr. Big, and Natasha—leaders of an international smuggling ring—had finally been caught!

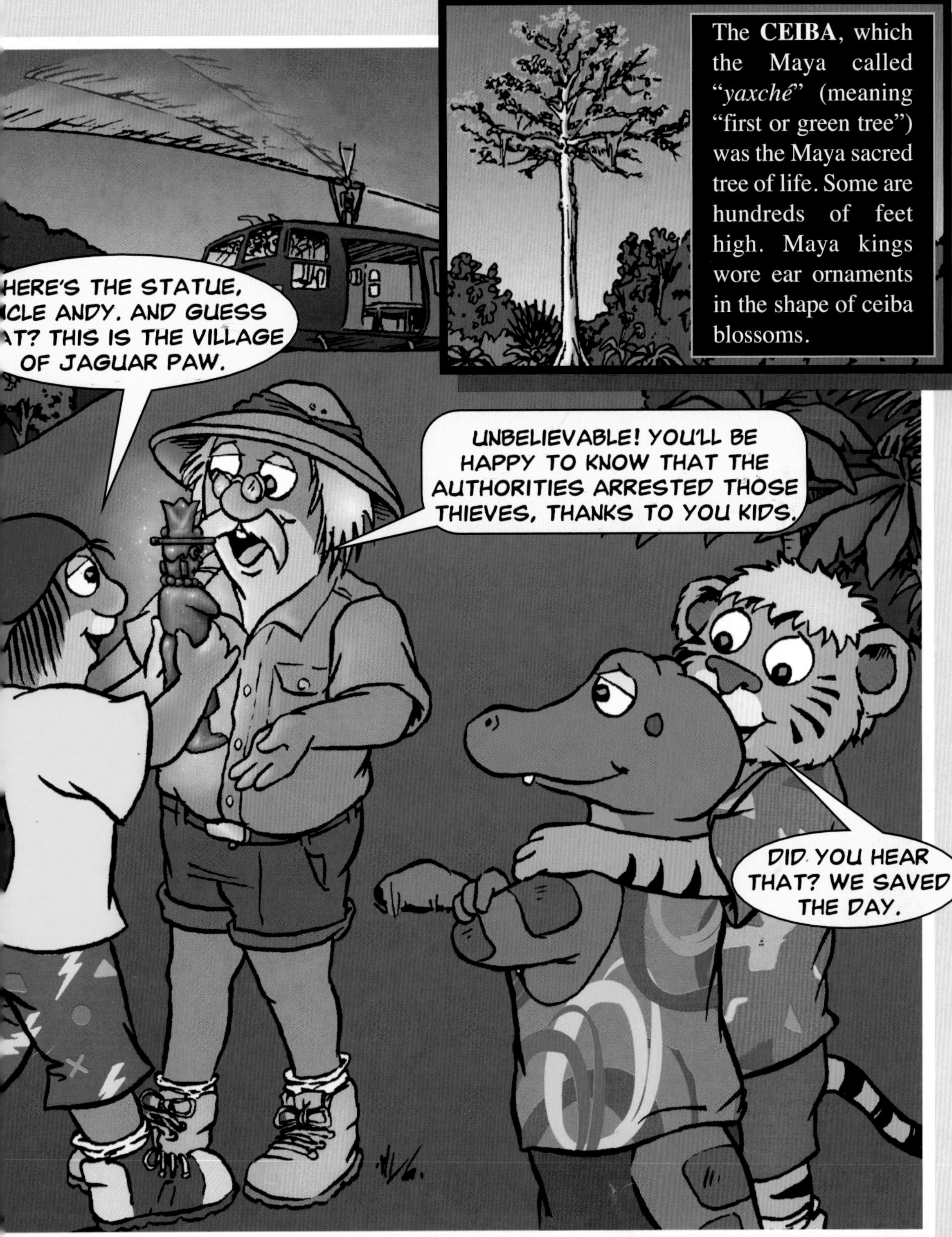

The **CEIBA**, which the Maya called "*yaxché*" (meaning "first or green tree") was the Maya sacred tree of life. Some are hundreds of feet high. Maya kings wore ear ornaments in the shape of ceiba blossoms.

HERE'S THE STATUE, CLE ANDY. AND GUESS AT? THIS IS THE VILLAGE OF JAGUAR PAW.
UNBELIEVABLE! YOU'LL BE HAPPY TO KNOW THAT THE AUTHORITIES ARRESTED THOSE THIEVES, THANKS TO YOU KIDS.
DID YOU HEAR THAT? WE SAVED THE DAY.

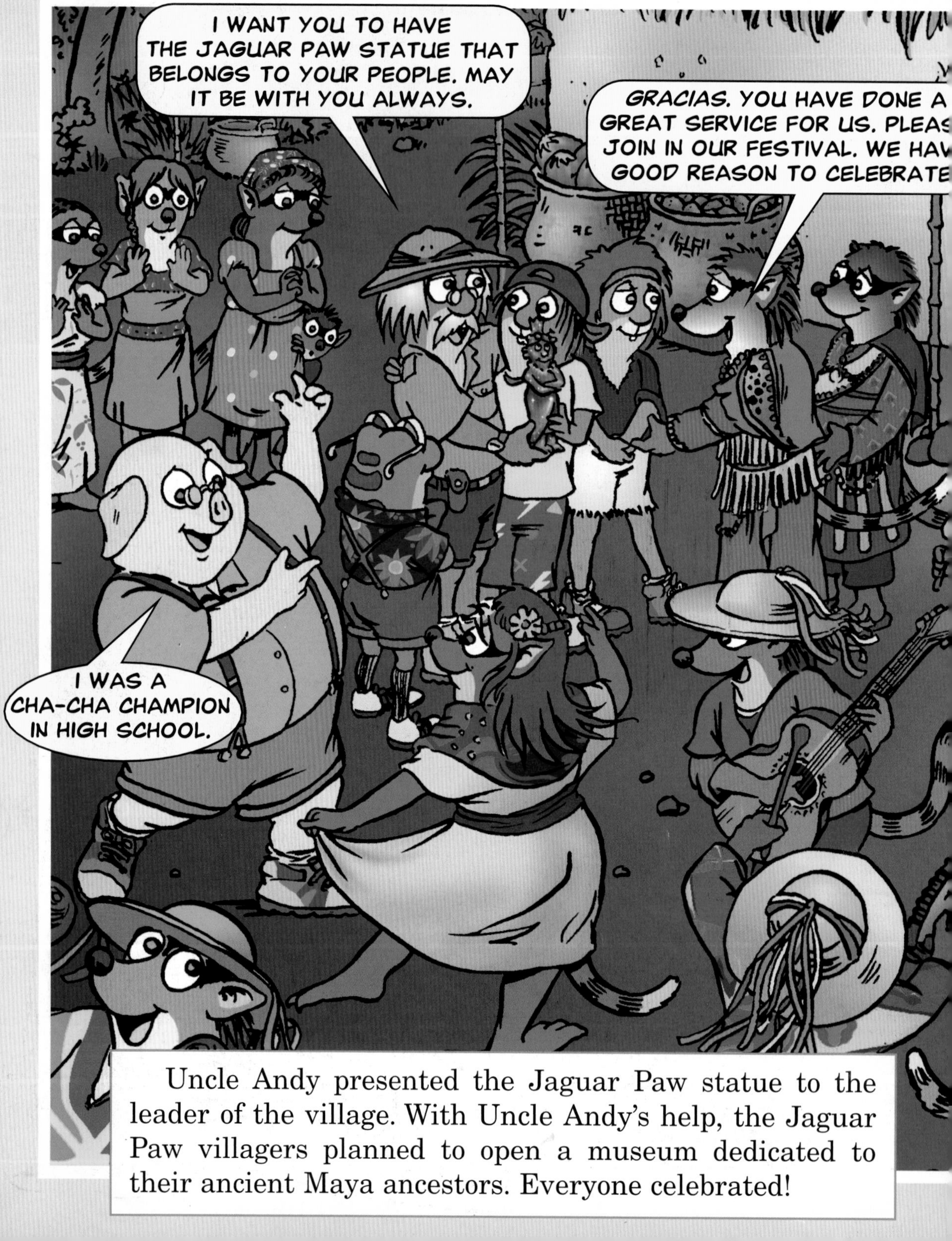
I WANT YOU TO HAVE THE JAGUAR PAW STATUE THAT BELONGS TO YOUR PEOPLE. MAY IT BE WITH YOU ALWAYS.
GRACIAS. YOU HAVE DONE A GREAT SERVICE FOR US. PLEAS JOIN IN OUR FESTIVAL. WE HAV GOOD REASON TO CELEBRATE
I WAS A CHA-CHA CHAMPION IN HIGH SCHOOL.

Uncle Andy presented the Jaguar Paw statue to the leader of the village. With Uncle Andy's help, the Jaguar Paw villagers planned to open a museum dedicated to their ancient Maya ancestors. Everyone celebrated!

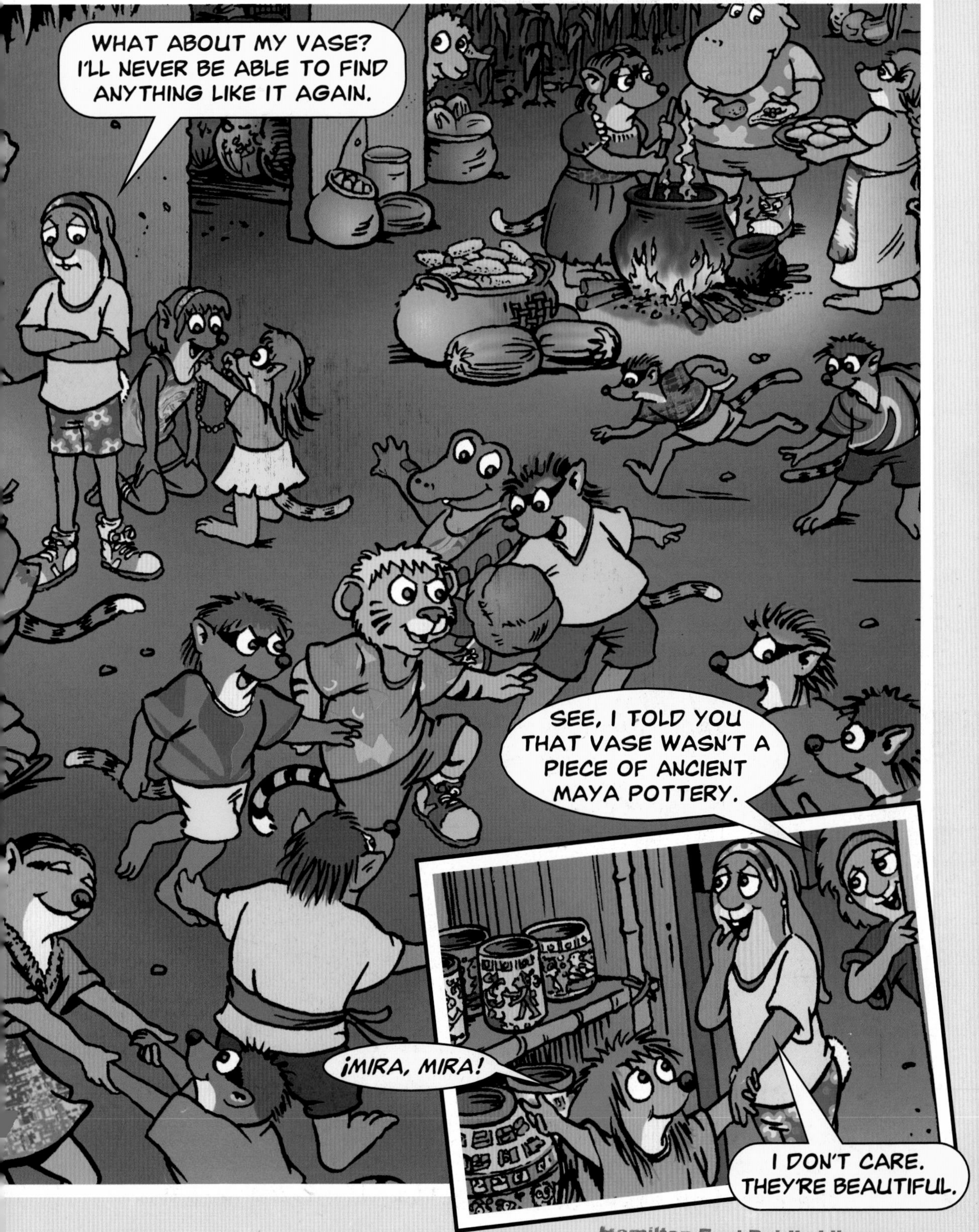
WHAT ABOUT MY VASE? I'LL NEVER BE ABLE TO FIND ANYTHING LIKE IT AGAIN.
SEE, I TOLD YOU THAT VASE WASN'T A PIECE OF ANCIENT MAYA POTTERY.
¡MIRA, MIRA!
I DON'T CARE. THEY'RE BEAUTIFUL.

Vocabulary

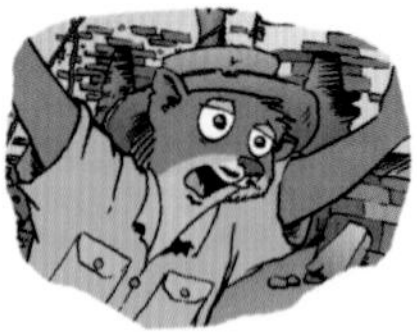

¡Ay caramba!—a Spanish phrase that means "Oh, no!" or "I can't believe it!"

¡Mira, mira!—a Spanish phrase that means "Look at this!"

a dig—a careful search through an area of land in order to find objects from long ago. *An archaeologist, like Uncle Andy, goes on a dig to look for ancient pottery or other objects to learn about people who lived long ago, such as the ancient Maya and the ancient Egyptians.*

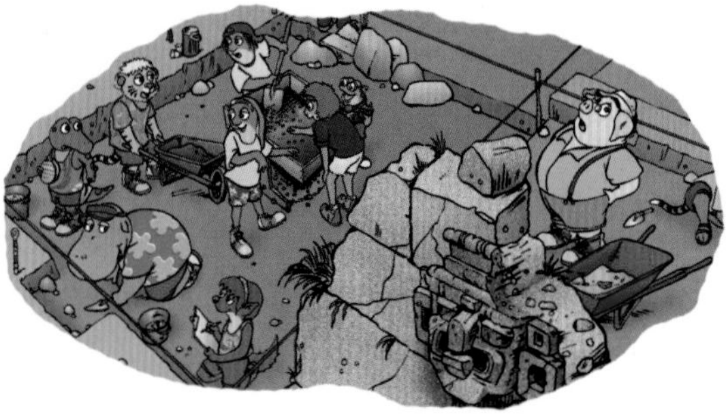

ancestors—family members that were born before your grandparents. *Finding the Jaguar Paw statue helped Uncle Andy learn about the Maya people's ancestors and how they lived long ago.*

archaeologist—a person who studies how people lived long ago by looking for the objects they may have left behind. *An archaeologist uses special tools when digging for objects.*

dynasty—several generations of an important and powerful group of people. *The villagers' ancestors were members of the Jaguar Paw dynasty.*

looted—stolen by sneaky means. *Mr. Big asked Squid if he had the looted statue.*

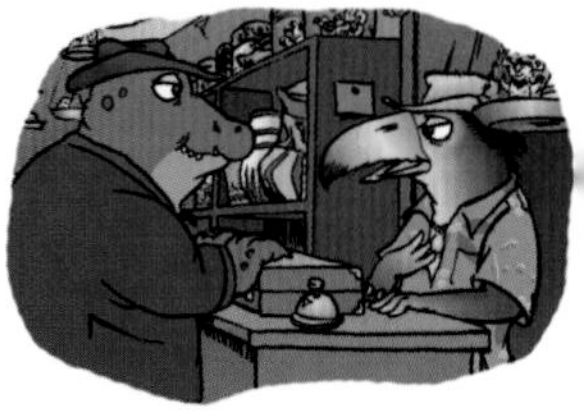

muchos pesos—Spanish for "a lot of money."

obsidian—black glass that forms when a volcano's hot lava cools quickly. *The Maya used pieces of obsidian for making spears for hunting.*

por favor—Spanish for "please."

turbulence—sudden, unstable gusts of wind. *Turbulence caused the airplane to bounce up and down through the sky.*

The Story and You

Who stole the Jaguar Paw statue? When and how was it stolen?

Why was it hard at first to figure out that Natasha was working with Squid and Mr. Big?

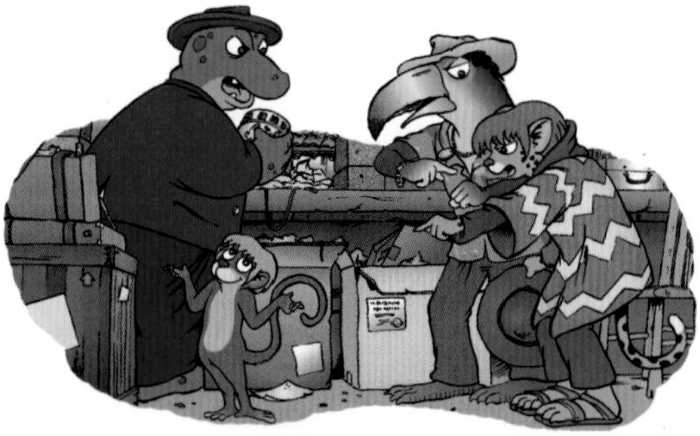

The Critter Kids got lucky several times in this story. Once was when Kiki picked up the other package. Describe another event that was lucky for them.

Su Su bought a vase as a souvenir of her trip to Tikal. If you had gone there with the Critter Kids, what souvenir would you buy? Why?